Stories of
Red Hanrahan

with The Secret Rose and Rosa Alchemica

William Butler Yeats

Dover Publications, Inc.
Mineola, New York

Bibliographical Note

This Dover edition, first published in 2013, is a newly reset, unabridged republication of the work originally published in 1914 by The Macmillan Company, New York.

Library of Congress Cataloging-in-Publication Data

Yeats, W. B. (William Butler), 1865-1939.
 [Short stories. Selections]
 Stories of Red Hanrahan : with The Secret Rose and Rosa Alchemica / W.B. Yeats.
— Dover edition.
       pages cm
 "This Dover edition, first published in 2013, is a newly reset, unabridged republication of the work originally published in 1914 by The Macmillan Company, New York"—T.p. verso.
 ISBN 978-0-486-49381-7 — ISBN 0-486-49381-4
 I. Title.
 PR5904.S76 2013
 823'.8—dc23

2013015588

Manufactured in the United States by Courier Corporation
49381401   2013
www.doverpublications.com

Contents

PAGE

STORIES OF RED HANRAHAN 1
Red Hanrahan 3
The Twisting of the Rope 12
Hanrahan and Cathleen the
    Daughter of Hoolihan 19
Red Hanrahan's Curse 23
Hanrahan's Vision 29
The Death of Hanrahan 34
Dedication to A. E. 40

THE SECRET ROSE 41
To the Secret Rose 45
The Crucifixion of the Outcast 47
Out of the Rose 55
The Wisdom of the King 61
The Heart of the Spring 67
The Curse of the Fires
    and of the Shadows 72
The Old Men of the Twilight 77
Where there is Nothing, there is God 81
Proud Costello, MacDermot's Daughter
    and the Bitter Tongue 85

ROSA ALCHEMICA 97

I owe thanks to Lady Gregory, who helped me to rewrite The Stories of Red Hanrahan *in the beautiful country speech of Kiltartan, and nearer to the tradition of the people among whom he, or some likeness of him, drifted and is remembered.*

STORIES OF RED HANRAHAN

RED HANRAHAN

HANRAHAN, THE HEDGE schoolmaster, a tall, strong, red-haired young man, came into the barn where some of the men of the village were sitting on Samhain Eve. It had been a dwelling-house, and when the man that owned it had built a better one, he had put the two rooms together, and kept it for a place to store one thing or another. There was a fire on the old hearth, and there were dip candles stuck in bottles, and there was a black quart bottle upon some boards that had been put across two barrels to make a table. Most of the men were sitting beside the fire, and one of them was singing a long wandering song, about a Munster man and a Connaught man that were quarreling about their two provinces.

Hanrahan went to the man of the house and said, "I got your message"; but when he had said that, he stopped, for an old mountainy man that had a shirt and trousers of unbleached flannel, and that was sitting by himself near the door, was looking at him, and moving an old pack of cards about in his hands and muttering. "Don't mind him," said the man of the house; "he is only some stranger came in awhile ago, and we bade him welcome, it being Samhain night, but I think he is not in his right wits. Listen to him now and you will hear what he is saying."

They listened then, and they could hear the old man muttering to himself as he turned the cards, "Spades and Diamonds, Courage and Power; Clubs and Hearts, Knowledge and Pleasure."

"That is the kind of talk he has been going on with for the last hour," said the man of the house, and Hanrahan turned his eyes from the old man as if he did not like to be looking at him.

3

"I got your message," Hanrahan said then; " 'he is in the barn with his three first cousins from Kilchriest,' the messenger said, 'and there are some of the neighbours with them.' "

"It is my cousin over there is wanting to see you," said the man of the house, and he called over a young frieze-coated man, who was listening to the song, and said, "This is Red Hanrahan you have the message for."

"It is a kind message, indeed," said the young man, "for it comes from your sweetheart, Mary Lavelle."

"How would you get a message from her, and what do you know of her?"

"I don't know her, indeed, but I was in Loughrea yesterday, and a neighbour of hers that had some dealings with me was saying that she bade him send you word, if he met anyone from this side in the market, that her mother has died from her, and if you have a mind yet to join with herself, she is willing to keep her word to you."

"I will go to her indeed," said Hanrahan.

"And she bade you make no delay, for if she has not a man in the house before the month is out, it is likely the little bit of land will be given to another."

When Hanrahan heard that, he rose up from the bench he had sat down on. "I will make no delay indeed," he said, "there is a full moon, and if I get as far as Gilchreist to-night, I will reach to her before the setting of the sun to-morrow."

When the others heard that, they began to laugh at him for being in such haste to go to his sweetheart, and one asked him if he would leave his school in the old lime-kiln, where he was giving the children such good learning. But he said the children would be glad enough in the morning to find the place empty, and no one to keep them at their task; and as for his school he could set it up again in any place, having as he had his little inkpot hanging from his neck by a chain, and his big Virgil and his primer in the skirt of his coat.

Some of them asked him to drink a glass before he went, and a young man caught hold of his coat, and said he must not leave them without singing the song he had made in praise of Venus and of Mary Lavelle. He drank a glass of whiskey, but he said he would not stop but would set out on his journey.

"There's time enough, Red Hanrahan," said the man of the house. "It will be time enough for you to give up sport when you are after your marriage, and it might be a long time before we will see you again."

"I will not stop," said Hanrahan; "my mind would be on the roads all the time, bringing me to the woman that sent for me, and she lonesome and watching till I come."

Some of the others came about him, pressing him that had been such a pleasant comrade, so full of songs and every kind of trick and fun, not to leave them till the night would be over, but he refused them all, and shook them off, and went to the door. But as he put his foot over the threshold, the strange old man stood up and put his hand that was thin and withered like a bird's claw on Hanrahan's hand, and said: "It is not Hanrahan, the learned man and the great songmaker, that should go out from a gathering like this, on a Samhain night. And stop here, now," he said, "and play a hand with me; and here is an old pack of cards has done its work many a night before this, and old as it is, there has been much of the riches of the world lost and won over it."

One of the young men said, "It isn't much of the riches of the world has stopped with yourself, old man," and he looked at the old man's bare feet, and they all laughed. But Hanrahan did not laugh, but he sat down very quietly, without a word. Then one of them said, "So you will stop with us after all, Hanrahan"; and the old man said: "He will stop indeed, did you not hear me asking him?"

They all looked at the old man then as if wondering where he came from. "It is far I am come," he said, "through France I have come, and through Spain, and by Lough Greine of the hidden mouth, and none has refused me anything." And then he was silent and nobody liked to question him, and they began to play. There were six men at the boards playing, and the others were looking on behind. They played two or three games for nothing, and then the old man took a fourpenny bit, worn very thin and smooth, out from his pocket, and he called to the rest to put something on the game. Then they all put down something on the boards, and little as it was it looked much, from the way it was shoved from one to another, first one man winning it and then his neighbour. And sometimes the luck would go against a man and he would have nothing left, and then one or another would lend him something, and he would pay it again out of his winnings, for neither good nor bad luck stopped long with anyone.

And once Hanrahan said as a man would say in a dream, "It is time for me to be going the road"; but just then a good card came to him, and he played it out, and all the money began to come to him. And once he thought of Mary Lavelle, and he sighed; and that time his luck went from him, and he forgot her again.

But at last the luck went to the old man and it stayed with him, and all they had flowed into him, and he began to laugh little laughs to himself, and to sing over and over to himself, "Spades and Diamonds, Courage and Power," and so on, as if it was a verse of a song.

And after a while anyone looking at the men, and seeing the way their bodies were rocking to and fro, and the way they kept their eyes on the old man's hands, would think they had drink taken, or that the whole store they had in the world was put on the cards; but that was not so, for the quart bottle had not been disturbed since the game began, and was nearly full yet, and all that was on the game was a few sixpenny bits and shillings, and maybe a handful of coppers.

"You are good men to win and good men to lose," said the old man, "you have play in your hearts." He began then to shuffle the cards and to mix them, very quick and fast, till at last they could not see them to be cards at all, but you would think him to be making rings of fire in the air, as little lads would make them with whirling a lighted stick; and after that it seemed to them that all the room was dark, and they could see nothing but his hands and the cards.

And all in a minute a hare made a leap out from between his hands, and whether it was one of the cards that took that shape, or whether it was made out of nothing in the palms of his hands, nobody knew, but there it was running on the floor of the barn, as quick as any hare that ever lived.

Some looked at the hare, but more kept their eyes on the old man, and while they were looking at him a hound made a leap out between his hands, the same way as the hare did, and after that another hound and another, till there was a whole pack of them following the hare round and round the barn.

The players were all standing up now, with their backs to the boards, shrinking from the hounds, and nearly deafened with the noise of their yelping, but as quick as the hounds were they could not overtake the hare, but it went round, till at the last it seemed as if a blast of wind burst open the barn door, and the hare doubled and made a leap over the boards where the men had been playing, and went out of the door and away through the night, and the hounds over the boards and through the doors after it.

Then the old man called out, "Follow the hounds, follow the hounds, and it is a great hunt you will see to-night," and he went out after them. But used as the men were to go hunting after hares, and ready as they were for any sport, they were in dread to go out into the night, and it was only Hanrahan that rose up and that said, "I will follow, I will follow on."

"You had best stop here, Hanrahan," the young man that was nearest him said, "for you might be going into some great danger." But Hanrahan said, "I will see fair play, I will see fair play," and he went stumbling out of the door like a man in a dream, and the door shut after him as he went.

He thought he saw the old man in front of him, but it was only his own shadow that the full moon cast on the road before him, but he could hear the hounds crying after the hare over the wide green fields of Granagh, and he followed them very fast for there was nothing to stop him; and after a while he came to smaller fields that had little walls of loose stones around them, and he threw the stones down as he crossed them, and did not wait to put them up again; and he passed by the place where the river goes under ground at Ballylee, and he could hear the hounds going before him up towards the head of the river. Soon he found it harder to run, for it was uphill he was going, and clouds came over the moon, and it was hard for him to see his way, and once he left the path to take a short cut, but his foot slipped into a bog-hole and he had to come back to it. And how long he was going he did not know, or what way he went, but at last he was up on the bare mountain, with nothing but the rough heather about him, and he could neither hear the hounds nor any other thing. But their cry began to come to him again, at first far off and then very near, and when it came quite close to him, it went up all of a sudden into the air, and there was the sound of hunting over his head; then it went away northward till he could hear nothing more at all. "That's not fair," he said, "that's not fair." And he could walk no longer, but sat down on the heather where he was, in the heart of Slieve Echtge, for all the strength had gone from him, with the dint of the long journey he had made.

And after a while he took notice that there was a door close to him, and a light coming from it, and he wondered that being so close to him he had not seen it before. And he rose up, and tired as he was he went in at the door, and although it was night time outside, it was daylight he found within. And presently he met with an old man that had been gathering summer thyme and yellow flag-flowers, and it seemed as if all the sweet smells of the summer were with them. And the old man said: "It is a long time you have been coming to us, Hanrahan the learned man and the great songmaker."

And with that he brought him into a very big shining house, and every grand thing Hanrahan had ever heard of, and every colour he had ever seen, were in it. There was a high place at the end of the house, and on it there was sitting in a high chair a woman, the most beautiful the world ever saw, having a long pale face and flowers about it, but she had the tired look of one that had been long waiting. And there was sitting on the step below her chair four grey old women, and the one of them was holding a great cauldron in her lap; and another a great stone on her knees, and heavy as it was it seemed light to her; and another of them had a very long spear that was made of pointed wood; and the last of them had a sword that was without a scabbard.

Hanrahan stood looking at them for a long time, but none of them spoke any word to him or looked at him at all. And he had it in his mind to ask who that woman in the chair was, that was like a queen, and what she was waiting for; but ready as he was with his tongue and afraid of no person, he was in dread now to speak to so beautiful a woman, and in so grand a place.

And then he thought to ask what were the four things the four grey old women were holding like great treasures, but he could not think of the right words to bring out.

Then the first of the old women rose up, holding the cauldron between her two hands, and she said "Pleasure," and Hanrahan said no word. Then the second old woman rose up with the stone in her hands, and she said "Power"; and the third old woman rose up with the spear in her hand, and she said "Courage"; and the last of the old women rose up having the sword in her hands, and she said "Knowledge." And everyone, after she had spoken, waited as if for Hanrahan to question her, but he said nothing at all. And then the four old women went out of the door, bringing their four treasures with them, and as they went out one of them said, "He has no wish for us"; and another said, "He is weak, he is weak"; and another said, "He is afraid"; and the last said, "His wits are gone from him." And then they all said, "Echtge, daughter of the Silver Hand, must stay in her sleep. It is a pity, it is a great pity."

And then the woman that was like a queen gave a very sad sigh, and it seemed to Hanrahan as if the sigh had the sound in it of hidden streams; and if the place he was in had been ten times grander and more shining than it was, he could not have hindered sleep from coming on him; and he staggered like a drunken man and lay down there and then.

When Hanrahan awoke, the sun was shining on his face, but there was white frost on the grass around him, and there was ice on the edge of the stream he was lying by, and that goes running on through Daire-caol and Druim-da-rod. He knew by the shape of the hills and by the shining of Lough Greine in the distance that he was upon one of the hills of Slieve Echtge, but he was not sure how he came there; for all that had happened in the barn had gone from him, and all of his journey but the soreness of his feet and the stiffness in his bones.

It was a year after that, there were men of the village of Cappaghtagle sitting by the fire in a house on the roadside, and Red Hanrahan that was now very thin and worn and his hair very long and wild, came to the half-door and asked leave to come in and rest himself; and they bid him welcome because it was Samhain night. He sat down with them, and they gave him a glass of whiskey out of a quart bottle; and they saw the little inkpot hanging about his neck, and knew he was a scholar, and asked for stories about the Greeks.

He took the Virgil out of the big pocket of his coat, but the cover was very black and swollen with the wet, and the page when he opened it was very yellow, but that was no great matter, for he looked at it like a man that had never learned to read. Some young man that was there began to laugh at him then, and to ask why did he carry so heavy a book with him when he was not able to read it.

It vexed Hanrahan to hear that, and he put the Virgil back in his pocket and asked if they had a pack of cards among them, for cards were better than books. When they brought out the cards he took them and began to shuffle them, and while he was shuffling them something seemed to come into his mind, and he put his hand to his face like one that is trying to remember, and he said: "Was I ever here before, or where was I on a night like this?" and then of a sudden he stood up and let the cards fall to the floor, and he said, "Who was it brought me a message from Mary Lavelle?"

"We never saw you before now, and we never heard of Mary Lavelle," said the man of the house. "And who is she," he said, "and what is it you are talking about?"

"It was this night a year ago, I was in a barn, and there were men playing cards, and there was money on the table, they were pushing it from one to another here and there—and I got a message, and I was going out of the door to look for my sweetheart that wanted me, Mary Lavelle." And then Hanrahan called out very loud: "Where have I been since then? Where was I for a whole year?"

"It is hard to say where you might have been in that time," said the oldest of the men, "or what part of the world you may have travelled; and it is like enough you have the dust of many roads on your feet; for there are many go wandering and forgetting like that," he said, "when once they have been given the touch."

"That is true," said another of the men. "I knew a woman went wandering like that through the length of seven years; she came back after, and she told her friends she had often been glad enough to eat the food that was put in the pig's trough. And it is best for you to go to the priest now," he said, "and let him take off you whatever may have been put upon you."

"It is to my sweetheart I will go, to Mary Lavelle," said Hanrahan; "it is too long I have delayed, how do I know what might have happened to her in the length of a year?"

He was going out of the door then, but they all told him it was best for him to stop the night, and to get strength for the journey; and indeed he wanted that, for he was very weak, and when they gave him food he eat it like a man that had never seen food before, and one of them said, "He is eating as if he had trodden on the hungry grass." It was in the white light of the morning he set out, and the time seemed long to him till he could get to Mary Lavelle's house. But when he came to it, he found the door broken, and the thatch dropping from the roof, and no living person to be seen. And when he asked the neighbours what had happened her, all they could say was that she had been put out of the house, and had married some labouring man, and they had gone looking for work to London or Liverpool or some big place. And whether she found a worse place or a better he never knew, but anyway he never met with her or with news of her again.

THE TWISTING OF THE ROPE

HANRAHAN WAS WALKING the roads one time near Kinvara at the fall of day, and he heard the sound of a fiddle from a house a little way off the roadside. He turned up the path to it, for he never had the habit of passing by any place where there was music or dancing or good company, without going in. The man of the house was standing at the door, and when Hanrahan came near he knew him and he said: "A welcome before you, Hanrahan, you have been lost to us this long time." But the woman of the house came to the door and she said to her husband: "I would be as well pleased for Hanrahan not to come in to-night, for he has no good name now among the priests, or with women that mind themselves, and I wouldn't wonder from his walk if he has a drop of drink taken." But the man said, "I will never turn away Hanrahan of the poets from my door," and with that he bade him enter.

There were a good many neighbours gathered in the house, and some of them remembered Hanrahan; but some of the little lads that were in the corners had only heard of him, and they stood up to have a view of him, and one of them said: "Is not that Hanrahan that had the school, and that was brought away by Them?" But his mother put her hand over his mouth and bade him be quiet, and not be saying things like that. "For Hanrahan is apt to grow wicked," she said, "if he hears talk of that story, or if anyone goes questioning him." One or another called out then, asking him for a song, but the man of the house said it was no time to ask him for a song, before he had rested himself; and he gave him whiskey in a glass, and Hanrahan thanked him and wished him good health and drank it off.

The fiddler was tuning his fiddle for another dance, and the man of the house said to the young men, they would all know what dancing was like when they saw Hanrahan dance, for the like of it had never been seen since he was there before. Hanrahan said he would not dance, he had better use for his feet now, travelling as he was through the five provinces of Ireland. Just as he said that, there came in at the half-door Oona, the daughter of the house, having a few bits of bog deal from Connemara in her arms for the fire. She threw them on the hearth and the flame rose up, and showed her to be very comely and smiling and two or three of the young men rose up and asked for a dance. But Hanrahan crossed the floor and brushed the others away, and said it was with him she must dance, after the long road he had travelled before he came to her. And it is likely he said some soft word in her ear, for she said nothing against it, and stood out with him, and there were little blushes in her cheeks. Then other couples stood up, but when the dance was going to begin, Hanrahan chanced to look down, and he took notice of his boots that were worn and broken, and the ragged grey socks showing through them; and he said angrily it was a bad floor, and the music no great things, and he sat down in the dark place beside the hearth. But if he did, the girl sat down there with him.

The dancing went on, and when that dance was over another was called for, and no one took much notice of Oona and Red Hanrahan for a while, in the corner where they were. But the mother grew to be uneasy, and she called to Oona to come and help her to set the table in the inner room. But Oona that had never refused her before, said she would come soon, but not yet, for she was listening to whatever he was saying in her ear. The mother grew yet more uneasy then, and she would come nearer them, and let on to be stirring the fire or sweeping the hearth, and she would listen for a minute to hear what the poet was saying to her child. And one time she heard him telling about white-handed Deirdre, and how she brought the sons of Usnach to their death; and how the blush in her cheeks was not so red as the blood of kings' sons that was shed for her, and her sorrows had never gone out of mind; and he said it was maybe the memory of her that made the cry of the plover on the bog as sorrowful in the ear of the poets as the keening of young men for a comrade. And there would never have been that memory of her, he said, if it was not for the poets that had put her beauty in their songs. And the next time she did not well understand what he was saying, but as far as she could hear, it had the sound of poetry though it was not rhymed, and this is what she heard him say: "The sun and the moon are the man and the girl, they are my life and your life, they are travelling and ever travelling through the skies as if under the one hood. It was God made them for one another. He made your life and my life before the beginning of the world, he made them that they might go through the world, up and down, like the two best dancers that go on with the dance up and down the long floor of the barn, fresh and laughing, when all the rest are tired out and leaning against the wall."

The old woman went then to where her husband was playing cards, but he would take no notice of her, and then she went to a woman of the neighbours and said: "Is there no way we can get them from one another?" and without waiting for an answer she said to some young men that were talking together: "What good are you when you cannot make the best girl in the house come out and dance with you? And go now the whole of you," she said, "and see can you bring her away from the poet's talk." But Oona would not listen to any of them, but only moved her hand as if to send them away. Then they called to Hanrahan and said he had best dance with the girl himself, or let her dance with one of them. When Hanrahan heard what they were saying he said: "That is so, I will dance with her; there is no man in the house must dance with her but myself."

He stood up with her then, and led her out by the hand, and some of the young men were vexed, and some began mocking at his ragged coat and his broken boots. But he took no notice, and Oona took no notice, but they looked at one another as if all the world belonged to themselves alone. But another couple that had been sitting together like lovers stood out on the floor at the same time, holding one another's hands and moving their feet to keep time with the music. But Hanrahan turned his back on them as if angry, and in place of dancing he began to sing, and as he sang he held her hand, and his voice grew louder, and the mocking of the young men stopped, and the fiddle stopped, and there was nothing heard but his voice that had in it the sound of the wind. And what he sang was a song he had heard or had made one time in his wanderings on Slieve Echtge, and the words of it as they can be put into English were like this:

O Death's old bony finger
Will never find us there
In the high hollow townland
Where love's to give and to spare;
Where boughs have fruit and blossom
At all times of the year;
Where rivers are running over
With red beer and brown beer.
An old man plays the bagpipes
In a gold and silver wood;
Queens, their eyes blue like the ice,
Are dancing in a crowd.

And while he was singing it Oona moved nearer to him, and the colour had gone from her cheek, and her eyes were not blue now, but grey with the tears that were in them, and any-one that saw her would have thought she was ready to follow him there and then from the west to the east of the world.

But one of the young men called out: "Where is that country he is singing about? Mind yourself, Oona, it is a long way off, you might be a long time on the road before you would reach to it." And another said: "It is not to the Country of the Young you will be going if you go with him, but to Mayo of the bogs." Oona looked at him then as if she would question him, but he raised her hand in his hand, and called out between sing-ing and shouting: "It is very near us that country is, it is on every side; it may be on the bare hill behind it is, or it may be in the heart of the wood." And he said out very loud and clear: "In the heart of the wood; oh, death will never find us in the heart of the wood. And will you come with me there, Oona?" he said.

But while he was saying this the two old women had gone outside the door, and Oona's mother was crying, and she said:

"He has put an enchantment on Oona. Can we not get the men to put him out of the house?"

"That is a thing you cannot do," said the other woman, "for he is a poet of the Gael, and you know well if you put a poet of the Gael out of the house, he would put a curse on you that would wither the corn in the fields and dry up the milk of the cows, if it had to hang in the air seven years."

"God help us," said the mother, "and why did I ever let him into the house at all, and the wild name he has!"

"It would have been no harm at all to have kept him outside, but there would be great harm come upon you if you put him out by force. But listen to the plan I have to get him out of the house by his own doing, without anyone putting him from it at all."

It was not long after that the two women came in again, each of them having a bundle of hay in her apron. Hanrahan was not singing now, but he was talking to Oona very fast and soft, and he was saying: "The house is narrow but the world is wide, and there is no true lover that need be afraid of night or morning or sun or stars or shadows of evening, or any earthly thing." "Hanrahan," said the mother then, striking him on the shoulder, "will you give me a hand here for a minute?" "Do that, Hanrahan," said the woman of the neighbours, "and help us to make this hay into a rope, for you are ready with your hands, and a blast of wind has loosened the thatch on the haystack."

"I will do that for you," said he, and he took the little stick in his hands, and the mother began giving out the hay, and he twisting it, but he was hurrying to have done with it, and to be free again. The women went on talking and giving out the hay, and encouraging him, and saying what a good twister of a rope he was, better than their own neighbours or than any one they had ever seen. And Hanrahan saw that Oona was watching him, and he began to twist very quick and with his head high, and to boast of the readiness of his hands, and the learning he had in his head, and the strength in his arms. And as he was boasting, he went backward, twisting the rope always till he came to the door that was open behind him, and without thinking he passed the threshold and was out on the road. And no sooner was he there than the mother made a sudden rush, and threw out the rope after him, and she shut the door and the half-door and put a bolt upon them.

She was well pleased when she had done that, and laughed out loud, and the neighbours laughed and praised her. But they heard him beating at the door, and saying words of cursing outside it, and the mother had but time to stop Oona that had her hand upon the bolt to open it. She made a sign to the fiddler then, and he began a reel, and one of the young men asked no leave but caught hold of Oona and brought her into the thick of the dance. And when it was over and the fiddle had stopped, there was no sound at all of anything outside, but the road was as quiet as before.

As to Hanrahan, when he knew he was shut out and that there was neither shelter nor drink nor a girl's ear for him that night, the anger and the courage went out of him, and he went on to where the waves were beating on the strand.

He sat down on a big stone, and he began swinging his right arm and singing slowly to himself, the way he did always to hearten himself when every other thing failed him. And whether it was that time or another time he made the song that is called to this day "The Twisting of the Rope," and that begins, "What was the dead cat that put me in this place," is not known.

But after he had been singing awhile, mist and shadows seemed to gather about him, sometimes coming out of the sea, and sometimes moving upon it. It seemed to him that one of the shadows was the queen-woman he had seen in her sleep at Slieve Echtge; not in her sleep now, but mocking, and calling out to them that were behind her: "He was weak, he was weak, he had no courage." And he felt the strands of the rope in his hand yet, and went on twisting it, but it seemed to him as he twisted, that it had all the sorrows of the world in it. And then it seemed to him as if the rope had changed in his dream into a great water-worm that came out of the sea, and that twisted itself about him, and held him closer and closer, and grew from big to bigger till the whole of the earth and skies were wound up in it, and the stars themselves were but the shining of the ridges of its skin. And then he got free of it, and went on, shaking and unsteady, along the edge of the strand, and the grey shapes were flying here and there around him. And this is what they were saying, "It is a pity for him that refuses the call of the daughters of the Sidhe, for he will find no comfort in the love of the women of the earth to the end of life and time, and the cold of the grave is in his heart for ever. It is death he has chosen; let him die, let him die, let him die."

HANRAHAN AND CATHLEEN
THE DAUGHTER OF HOOLIHAN

IT WAS TRAVELLING northward Hanrahan was one time, giving a hand to a farmer now and again in the hurried time of the year, and telling his stories and making his share of songs at wakes and at weddings.

He chanced one day to overtake on the road to Collooney one Margaret Rooney, a woman he used to know in Munster when he was a young man. She had no good name at that time, and it was the priest routed her out of the place at last. He knew her by her walk and by the colour of her eyes, and by a way she had of putting back the hair off her face with her left hand. She had been wandering about, she said, selling herrings and the like, and now she was going back to Sligo, to the place in the Burrough where she was living with another woman, Mary Gillis, who had much the same story as herself. She would be well pleased, she said, if he would come and stop in the house with them, and be singing his songs to the bacachs and blind men and fiddlers of the Burrough. She remembered him well, she said, and had a wish for him; and as to Mary Gillis, she had some of his songs off by heart, so he need not be afraid of not getting good treatment, and all the bacachs and poor men that heard him would give him a share of their own earnings for his stories and his songs while he was with them, and would carry his name into all the parishes of Ireland.

He was glad enough to go with her, and to find a woman to be listening to the story of his troubles and to be comforting him. It was at the moment of the fall of day when every man may pass as handsome and every woman as comely. She put her arm about him when he told her of the misfortune of the Twisting of the Rope, and in the half light she looked as well as another.

They kept in talk all the way to the Burrough, and as for Mary Gillis, when she saw him and heard who he was, she went near crying to think of having a man with so great a name in the house.

Hanrahan was well pleased to settle down with them for a while, for he was tired with wandering; and since the day he found the little cabin fallen in, and Mary Lavelle gone from it, and the thatch scattered, he had never asked to have any place of his own; and he had never stopped long enough in any place to see the green leaves come where he had seen the old leaves wither, or to see the wheat harvested where he had seen it sown. It was a good change to him to have shelter from the wet, and a fire in the evening time, and his share of food put on the table without the asking.

He made a good many of his songs while he was living there, so well cared for and so quiet. The most of them were love songs, but some were songs of repentance, and some were songs about Ireland and her griefs, under one name or another.

Every evening the bacachs and beggars and blind men and fiddlers would gather into the house and listen to his songs and his poems, and his stories about the old time of the Fianna, and they kept them in their memories that were never spoiled with books; and so they brought his name to every wake and wedding and pattern in the whole of Connaught. He was never so well off or made so much of as he was at that time.

One evening of December he was singing a little song that he said he had heard from the green plover of the mountain, about the fair-haired boys that had left Limerick, and that were wandering and going astray in all parts of the world. There were a good many people in the room that night, and two or three little lads that had crept in, and sat on the floor near the fire, and were too busy with the roasting of a potato in the ashes or some such thing to take much notice of him; but they remembered long afterwards when his name had gone up, the sound of his voice, and what way he had moved his hand, and the look of him as he sat on the edge of the bed, with his shadow falling on the whitewashed wall behind him, and as he moved going up as high as the thatch. And they knew then that they had looked upon a king of the poets of the Gael, and a maker of the dreams of men.

Of a sudden his singing stopped, and his eyes grew misty as if he was looking at some far thing.

Mary Gillis was pouring whiskey into a mug that stood on a table beside him, and she left off pouring and said, "Is it of leaving us you are thinking?"

Margaret Rooney heard what she said, and did not know why she said it, and she took the words too much in earnest and came over to him, and there was dread in her heart that she was going to lose so wonderful a poet and so good a comrade, and a man that was thought so much of, and that brought so many to her house.

"You would not go away from us, my heart?" she said, catching him by the hand.

"It is not of that I am thinking," he said, "but of Ireland and the weight of grief that is on her." And he leaned his head against his hand, and began to sing these words, and the sound of his voice was like the wind in a lonely place.

The old brown thorn trees break in two high over Cummen
    Strand.
Under a bitter black wind that blows from the left hand;
Our courage breaks like an old tree in a black wind and dies,
But we have hidden in our hearts the flame out of the eyes
Of Cathleen the daughter of Hoolihan.

The winds was bundled up the clouds high over Knocknarea
And thrown the thunder on the stones for all that Maeve can
    say;
Angers that are like noisy clouds have set our hearts abeat,
But we have all bent low and low and kissed the quiet feet
Of Cathleen the daughter of Hoolihan

The yellow pool has overflowed high up on Cloothna-Bare,
For the wet winds are blowing out of the clinging air;
Like heavy flooded waters our bodies and our blood,
But purer than a tall candle before the Holy Rood
Is Cathleen the daughter of Hoolihan.

While he was singing, his voice began to break, and tears came rolling down his cheeks, and Margaret Rooney put down her face into her hands and began to cry along with him. Then a blind beggar by the fire shook his rags with a sob, and after that there was no one of them all but cried tears down.

RED HANRAHAN'S CURSE

ONE FINE MAY morning a long time after Hanrahan had left Margaret Rooney's house, he was walking the road near Collooney, and the sound of the birds singing in the bushes that were white with blossom set him singing as he went. It was to his own little place he was going, that was no more than a cabin, but that pleased him well. For he was tired of so many years of wandering from shelter to shelter at all times of the year, and although he was seldom refused a welcome and a share of what was in the house, it seemed to him sometimes that his mind was getting stiff like his joints, and it was not so easy to him as it used to be to make fun and sport through the night, and to set all the boys laughing with his pleasant talk, and to coax the women with his songs. And a while ago, he had turned into a cabin that some poor man had left to go harvesting and had never come to again. And when he had mended the thatch and made a bed in the corner with a few sacks and bushes, and had swept out the floor, he was well content to have a little place for himself, where he could go in and out as he liked, and put his head in his hands through the length of an evening if the fret was on him, and loneliness after the old times. One by one the neighbours began to send their children in to get some learning from him, and with what they brought, a few eggs, or an oaten cake or a couple of sods of turf, he made out a way of living. And if he went for a wild day and night now and again to the Burrough, no one would say a word, knowing him to be a poet, with wandering in his heart.

It was from the Burrough he was coming that May morning, light-hearted enough, and singing some new song that had come to him. But it was not long till a hare ran across his path, and made away into the fields, through the loose stones of the wall. And he knew it was no good sign a hare to have crossed his path, and he remembered the hare that had led him away to Slieve Echtge the time Mary Lavelle was waiting for him, and how he had never known content for any length of time since then. "And it is likely enough they are putting some bad thing before me now," he said.

And after he said that he heard the sound of crying in the field beside him, and he looked over the wall. And there he saw a young girl sitting under a bush of white hawthorn, and crying as if her heart would break. Her face was hidden in her hands, but her soft hair and her white neck and the young look of her, put him in mind of Bridget Purcell and Margaret Gillane and Maeve Connelan and Oona Curry and Celia Driscoll, and the rest of the girls he had made songs for and had coaxed the heart from with his flattering tongue.

She looked up, and he saw her to be a girl of the neighbours, a farmer's daughter. "What is on you, Nora?" he said. "Nothing you could take from me, Red Hanrahan." "If there is any sorrow on you it is I myself should be well able to serve you," he said then, "for it is I know the history of the Greeks, and I know well what sorrow is and parting, and the hardship of the world. And if I am not able to save you from trouble," he said, "there is many a one I have saved from it with the power that is in my songs, as it was in the songs of the poets that were before me from the beginning of the world. And it is with the rest of the poets I myself will be sitting and talking in some far place beyond the world, to the end of life and time," he said. The girl stopped her crying, and she said, "Owen Hanrahan, I often heard you have had sorrow and persecution, and that you know all the troubles of the world since the time you refused your love to the queen-woman in Slieve Echtge; and that she never left you in quiet since. But when it is people of this earth that have harmed you, it is yourself knows well the way to put harm on them again. And will you do now what I ask you, Owen Hanrahan?" she said. "I will do that indeed," said he.

"It is my father and my mother and my brothers," she said, "that are marrying me to old Paddy Doe, because he has a farm of a hundred acres under the mountain. And it is what you can do, Hanrahan," she said, "put him into a rhyme the same way you put old Peter Kilmartin in one the time you were young, that sorrow may be over him rising up and lying down, that will put him thinking of Collooney churchyard and not of marriage. And let you make no delay about it, for it is for to-morrow they have the marriage settled, and I would sooner see the sun rise on the day of my death than on that day."

"I will put him into a song that will bring shame and sorrow over him; but tell me how many years has he, for I would put them in the song?"

"O, he has years upon years. He is as old as you yourself, Red Hanrahan." "As old as myself," said Hanrahan, and his voice was as if broken; "as old as myself; there are twenty years and more between us! It is a bad day indeed for Owen Hanrahan when a young girl with the blossom of May in her cheeks thinks him to be an old man. And my grief!" he said, "you have put a thorn in my heart."

He turned from her then and went down the road till he came to a stone, and he sat down on it, for it seemed as if all the weight of the years had come on him in the minute. And he remembered it was not many days ago that a woman in some house had said: "It is not Red Hanrahan you are now but yellow Hanrahan, for your hair is turned to the colour of a wisp of tow." And another woman he had asked for a drink had not given him new milk but sour; and sometimes the girls would be whispering and laughing with young ignorant men while he himself was in the middle of giving out his poems or his talk. And he thought of the stiffness of his joints when he first rose of a morning, and the pain of his knees after making a journey, and it seemed to him as if he was come to be a very old man, with cold in the shoulders and speckled shins and his wind breaking and he himself withering away. And with those thoughts there came on him a great anger against old age and all it brought with it. And just then he looked up and saw a great spotted eagle sailing slowly towards Ballygawley, and he cried out: "You, too, eagle of Ballygawley, are old, and your wings are full of gaps, and I will put you and your ancient comrades, the Pike of Dargan Lake and the Yew of the Steep Place of the Strangers into my rhyme, that there may be a curse on you for ever."

There was a bush beside him to the left, flowering like the rest, and a little gust of wind blew the white blossoms over his coat. "May blossoms," he said, gathering them up in the hollow of his hand, "you never know age because you die away in your beauty, and I will put you into my rhyme and give you my blessing."

He rose up then and plucked a little branch from the bush, and carried it in his hand. But it is old and broken he looked going home that day with the stoop in his shoulders and the darkness in his face.

When he got to his cabin there was no one there, and he went and lay down on the bed for a while as he was used to do when he wanted to make a poem or a praise or a curse. And it was not long he was in making it this time, for the power of the curse-making bards was upon him. And when he had made it he searched his mind how he could send it out over the whole countryside.

Some of the scholars began coming in then, to see if there would be any school that day, and Hanrahan rose up and sat on the bench by the hearth, and they all stood around him.

They thought he would bring out the Virgil or the Mass book or the primer, but instead of that he held up the little branch of hawthorn he had in his hand yet. "Children," he said, "this is a new lesson I have for you to-day.

"You yourselves and the beautiful people of the world are like this blossom, and old age is the wind that comes and blows the blossom away. And I have made a curse upon old age and upon the old men, and listen now while I give it out to you." And this is what he said,—

> The poet, Owen Hanrahan, under a bush of may
> Calls down a curse on his own head because it withers grey;
> Then on the speckled eagle cock of Ballygawley Hill,
> Because it is the oldest thing that knows of cark and ill;
> And on the yew that has been green from the times out of
>   mind
> By the Steep Place of the Strangers and the Gap of the Wind;

And on the great grey pike that broods in Castle Dargan Lake
Having in his long body a many a hook and ache;
Then curses he old Paddy Bruen of the Well of Bride
Because no hair is on his head and drowsiness inside.
Then Paddy's neighbour, Peter Hart, and Michael Gill, his
    friend,
Because their wandering histories are never at an end.
And then old Shemus Cullinan, shepherd of the Green Lands
Because he holds two crutches between his crooked hands;
Then calls a curse from the dark North upon old Paddy Doe,
Who plans to lay his withering head upon a breast of snow,
Who plans to wreck a singing voice and break a merry heart,
He bids a curse hang over him till breath and body part;
But he calls down a blessing on the blossom of the may,
Because it comes in beauty, and in beauty blows away.

He said it over to the children verse by verse till all of them
could say a part of it, and some that were the quickest could say
the whole of it.

"That will do for to-day," he said then. "And what you have
to do now is to go out and sing that song for a while, to the
tune of the Green Bunch of Rushes, to everyone you meet,
and to the old men themselves."

"I will do that," said one of the little lads; "I know old Paddy
Doe well. Last Saint John's Eve we dropped a mouse down his
chimney, but this is better than a mouse."

"I will go into the town of Sligo and sing it in the street," said
another of the boys. "Do that," said Hanrahan, "and go into the
Burrough and tell it to Margaret Rooney and Mary Gillis, and
bid them sing it, and to make the beggars and the bacachs sing
it wherever they go." The children ran out then, full of pride
and of mischief, calling out the song as they ran, and Hanrahan
knew there was no danger it would not be heard.

He was sitting outside the door the next morning, looking at
his scholars as they came by in twos and threes. They were
nearly all come, and he was considering the place of the sun in
the heavens to know whether it was time to begin, when he
heard a sound that was like the buzzing of a swarm of bees in
the air, or the rushing of a hidden river in time of flood. Then
he saw a crowd coming up to the cabin from the road, and he

took notice that all the crowd was made up of old men, and that the leaders of it were Paddy Bruen, Michael Gill and Paddy Doe, and there was not one in the crowd but had in his hand an ash stick or a blackthorn. As soon as they caught sight of him, the sticks began to wave hither and thither like branches in a storm, and the old feet to run.

He waited no longer, but made off up the hill behind the cabin till he was out of their sight.

After a while he came back round the hill, where he was hidden by the furze growing along a ditch. And when he came in sight of his cabin he saw that all the old men had gathered around it, and one of them was just at that time thrusting a rake with a wisp of lighted straw on it into the thatch.

"My grief," he said, "I have set Old Age and Time and Weariness and Sickness against me, and I must go wandering again. And, O Blessed Queen of Heaven," he said, "protect me from the Eagle of Ballygawley, the Yew Tree of the Steep Place of the Strangers, the Pike of Castle Dargan Lake, and from the lighted wisps of their kindred, the Old Men!"

HANRAHAN'S VISION

IT WAS IN the month of June Hanrahan was on the road near Sligo, but he did not go into the town, but turned towards Ben Bulben; for there were thoughts of the old times coming upon him, and he had no mind to meet with common men. And as he walked he was singing to himself a song that had come to him one time in his dreams:

> O Death's old bony finger
> Will never find us there
> In the high hollow townland
> Where love's to give and to spare;
> Where boughs have fruit and blossom
> At all times of the year;
> Where rivers are running over
> With red beer and brown beer.
> An old man plays the bagpipes
> In a gold and silver wood;
> Queens, their eyes blue like the ice,
> Are dancing in a crowd.
>
> The little fox he murmured,
> "O what of the world's bane?"
> The sun was laughing sweetly,
> The moon plucked at my rein;
> But the little red fox murmured,
> "O do not pluck at his rein,
> He is riding to the townland
> That is the world's bane."
>
> When their hearts are so high
> That they would come to blows,

29

They unhook their heavy swords
From golden and silver boughs:
But all that are killed in battle
Awaken to life again:
It is lucky that their story
Is not known among men.
For O, the strong farmers
That would let the spade lie,
Their hearts would be like a cup
That somebody had drunk dry.

Michael will unhook his trumpet
From a bough overhead,
And blow a little noise
When the supper has been spread.
Gabriel will come from the water
With a fish tail, and talk
Of wonders that have happened
On wet roads where men walk,
And lift up an old horn
Of hammered silver, and drink
Till he has fallen asleep
Upon the starry brink.

Hanrahan had begun to climb the mountain then, and he gave over singing, for it was a long climb for him, and every now and again he had to sit down and to rest for a while. And one time he was resting he took notice of a wild briar bush, with blossoms on it, that was growing beside a rath, and it brought to mind the wild roses he used to bring to Mary Lavelle, and to no woman after her. And he tore off a little branch of the bush, that had buds on it and open blossoms, and he went on with his song:

The little fox he murmured,
"O what of the world's bane?"
The sun was laughing sweetly,
The moon plucked at my rein;
But the little red fox murmured,
"O do not pluck at his rein,
He is riding to the townland
That is the world's bane."

And he went on climbing the hill, and left the rath, and there came to his mind some of the old poems that told of lovers, good and bad, and of some that were awakened from the sleep of the grave itself by the strength of one another's love, and brought away to a life in some shadowy place, where they are waiting for the judgment and banished from the face of God.

And at last, at the fall of day, he came to the Steep Place of the Strangers, and there he laid himself down along a ridge of rock, and looked into the valley, that was full of grey mist spreading from mountain to mountain.

And it seemed to him as he looked that the mist changed to shapes of shadowy men and women, and his heart began to beat with the fear and the joy of the sight. And his hands, that were always restless, began to pluck off the leaves of the roses on the little branch, and he watched them as they went floating down into the valley in a little fluttering troop.

Suddenly he heard a faint music, a music that had more laughter in it and more crying than all the music of this world. And his heart rose when he heard that, and he began to laugh out loud, for he knew that music was made by some who had a beauty and a greatness beyond the people of this world. And it seemed to him that the little soft rose leaves as they went fluttering down into the valley began to change their shape till they looked like a troop of men and women far off in the mist, with the colour of the roses on them. And then that colour changed to many colours, and what he saw was a long line of tall beautiful young men, and of queen-women, that were not going from him but coming towards him and past him, and their faces were full of tenderness for all their proud looks, and were very pale and worn, as if they were seeking and ever seeking for high sorrowful things. And shadowy arms were stretched out of the mist as if to take hold of them, but could not touch them, for the quiet that was about them could not be broken. And before them and beyond them, but at a distance as if in reverence, there were other shapes, sinking and rising and coming and going, and Hanrahan knew them by their whirling flight to be the Sidhe, the ancient defeated gods; and the shadowy arms did not rise to take hold of them, for they were of those that can neither sin nor obey. And they all lessened then in the distance, and they seemed to be going towards the white door that is in the side of the mountain.

The mist spread out before him now like a deserted sea washing the mountains with long grey waves, but while he was looking at it, it began to fill again with a flowing broken witless life that was a part of itself, and arms and pale heads covered with tossing hair appeared in the greyness. It rose higher and higher till it was level with the edge of the steep rock, and then the shapes grew to be solid, and a new procession half lost in mist passed very slowly with uneven steps, and in the midst of each shadow there was something shining in the starlight. They came nearer and nearer, and Hanrahan saw that they also were lovers, and that they had heart-shaped mirrors instead of hearts, and they were looking and ever looking on their own faces in one another's mirrors. They passed on, sinking downward as they passed, and other shapes rose in their place, and these did not keep side by side, but followed after one another, holding out wild beckoning arms, and he saw that those who were followed were women, and as to their heads they were beyond all beauty, but as to their bodies they were but shadows without life, and their long hair was moving and trembling about them, as if it lived with some terrible life of its own. And then the mist rose of a sudden and hid them, and then a light gust of wind blew them away towards the north-east, and covered Hanrahan at the same time with a white wing of cloud.

He stood up trembling and was going to turn away from the valley, when he saw two dark and half-hidden forms standing as if in the air just beyond the rock, and one of them that had the sorrowful eyes of a beggar said to him in a woman's voice, "Speak to me, for no one in this world or any other world has spoken to me for seven hundred years."

"Tell me who are those that have passed by," said Hanrahan.

"Those that passed first," the woman said, "are the lovers that had the greatest name in the old times, Blanad and Deirdre and Grania and their dear comrades, and a great many that are not so well known but are as well loved. And because it was not only the blossom of youth they were looking for in one another, but the beauty that is as lasting as the night and the stars, the night and the stars hold them for ever from the warring and the perishing, in spite of the wars and the bitterness their love brought into the world. And those that came next," she said, "and that still breathe the sweet air and have the mirrors in their hearts, are not put in songs by the poets, because they sought only to triumph one over the other, and so to prove their strength and beauty, and out of this they made a kind of love. And as to the women with shadow-bodies, they desired neither to triumph nor to love but only to be loved, and there is no blood in their hearts or in their bodies until it flows through them from a kiss, and their life is but for a moment. All these are unhappy, but I am the unhappiest of all, for I am Dervadilla, and this is Dermot, and it was our sin brought the Norman into Ireland. And the curses of all the generations are upon us, and none are punished as we are punished. It was but the blossom of the man and of the woman we loved in one another, the dying beauty of the dust and not the everlasting beauty. When we died there was no lasting unbreakable quiet about us, and the bitterness of the battles we brought into Ireland turned to our own punishment. We go wandering together for ever, but Dermot that was my lover sees me always as a body that has been a long time in the ground, and I know that is the way he sees me. Ask me more, ask me more, for all the years have left their wisdom in my heart, and no one has listened to me for seven hundred years."

A great terror had fallen upon Hanrahan, and lifting his arms above his head he screamed out loud three times, and the cattle in the valley lifted their heads and lowed, and the birds in the wood at the edge of the mountain awaked out of their sleep and fluttered through the trembling leaves. But a little below the edge of the rock, the troop of rose leaves still fluttered in the air, for the gateway of Eternity had opened and shut again in one beat of the heart.

THE DEATH OF HANRAHAN

HANRAHAN, THAT WAS never long in one place, was back again among the villages that are at the foot of Slieve Echtge, Illeton and Scalp and Ballylee, stopping sometimes in one house and sometimes in another, and finding a welcome in every place for the sake of the old times and of his poetry and his learning. There was some silver and some copper money in the little leather bag under his coat, but it was seldom he needed to take anything from it, for it was little he used, and there was not one of the people that would have taken payment from him. His hand had grown heavy on the blackthorn he leaned on, and his cheeks were hollow and worn, but so far as food went, potatoes and milk and a bit of oaten cake, he had what he wanted of it; and it is not on the edge of so wild and boggy a place as Echtge a mug of spirits would be wanting, with the taste of the turf smoke on it. He would wander about the big wood at Kinadife, or he would sit through many hours of the day among the rushes about Lake Belshragh, listening to the streams from the hills, or watching the shadows in the brown bog pools; sitting so quiet as not to startle the deer that came down from the heather to the grass and the tilled fields at the fall of night. As the days went by it seemed as if he was beginning to belong to some world out of sight and misty, that has for its mearing the colours that are beyond all other colours and the silences that are beyond all silences of this world. And sometimes he would hear coming and going in the wood music that when it stopped went from his memory like a dream; and once in the stillness of midday he heard a sound like the clashing of many swords, that went on for a long time without any break. And at the fall of night and at moonrise the lake would grow to be like a gateway of silver and shining stones, and there would come from its silence the faint sound of keening and of frightened laughter broken by the wind, and many pale beckoning hands.

He was sitting looking into the water one evening in harvest time, thinking of all the secrets that were shut into the lakes and the mountains, when he heard a cry coming from the south, very faint at first, but getting louder and clearer as the shadow of the rushes grew longer, till he could hear the words, "I am beautiful, I am beautiful; the birds in the air, the moths under the leaves, the flies over the water look at me, for they never saw any one so beautiful as myself. I am young; I am young: look upon me, mountains; look upon me, perishing woods, for my body will shine like the white waters when you have been hurried away. You and the whole race of men, and the race of the beasts and the race of the fish and the winged race are dropping like a candle that is nearly burned out, but I laugh out because I am in my youth." The voice would break off from time to time, as if tired, and then it would begin again, calling out always the same words, "I am beautiful, I am beautiful." Presently the bushes at the edge of the little lake trembled for a moment, and a very old woman forced her way among them, and passed by Hanrahan, walking with very slow steps. Her face was the colour of earth, and more wrinkled than the face of any old hag that was ever seen, and her grey hair was hanging in wisps, and the rags she was wearing did not hide her dark skin that was roughened by all weathers. She passed by him with her eyes wide open, and her head high, and her arms hanging straight beside her, and she went into the shadow of the hills towards the west.

A sort of dread came over Hanrahan when he saw her, for he knew her to be one Winny Byrne, that went begging from place to place crying always the same cry, and he had often heard that she had once such wisdom that all the women of the neighbours used to go looking for advice from her, and that she had a voice so beautiful that men and women would come from every part to hear her sing at a wake or a wedding; and that the Others, the great Sidhe, had stolen her wits one Samhain night many years ago, when she had fallen asleep on the edge of a rath, and he had seen in her dreams the servants of Echtge of the hills.

And as she vanished away up the hillside, it seemed as if her cry, "I am beautiful, I am beautiful," was coming from among the stars in the heavens.

There was a cold wind creeping among the rushes, and Hanrahan began to shiver, and he rose up to go to some house where there would be a fire on the hearth. But instead of turning down the hill as he was used, he went on up the hill, along the little track that was maybe a road and maybe the dry bed of a stream. It was the same way Winny had gone, and it led to the little cabin where she stopped when she stopped in any place at all. He walked very slowly up the hill as if he had a great load on his back, and at last he saw a light a little to the left, and he thought it likely it was from Winny's house it was shining, and he turned from the path to go to it. But clouds had come over the sky, and he could not well see his way, and after he had gone a few steps his foot slipped and he fell into a bog drain, and though he dragged himself out of it, holding on to the roots of the heather, the fall had given him a great shake, and he felt better fit to lie down than to go travelling. But he had always great courage, and he made his way on, step by step, till at last he came to Winny's cabin, that had no window, but the light was shining from the door. He thought to go into it and to rest for a while, but when he came to the door he did not see Winny inside it, but what he saw was four old grey-haired women playing cards, but Winny herself was not among them. Hanrahan sat down on a heap of turf beside the door, for he was tired out and out, and had no wish for talking or for card-playing, and his bones and his joints aching the way they were. He could hear the four women talking as they played, and calling out their hands. And it seemed to him that they were saying, like the strange man in the barn long ago: "Spades and Diamonds, Courage and Power. Clubs and Hearts, Knowledge and Pleasure." And he went on saying those words over and over to himself; and whether or not he was in his dreams, the pain that was in his shoulder never left him. And after a while the four women in the cabin began to quarrel, and each one to say the other had not played fair, and their voices grew from loud to louder, and their screams and their curses, till at last the whole air was filled with the noise of them around and above the house, and Hanrahan, hearing it between sleep and waking, said: "That is the sound of the fighting between the friends and the ill-wishers of a man that is near his death. And I wonder," he said, "who is the man in this lonely place that is near his death."

It seemed as if he had been asleep a long time, and he opened his eyes, and the face he saw over him was the old wrinkled face of Winny of the Cross Road. She was looking hard at him, as if to make sure he was not dead, and she wiped away the blood that had grown dry on his face with a wet cloth, and after a while she partly helped him and partly lifted him into the cabin, and laid him down on what served her for a bed. She gave him a couple of potatoes from a pot on the fire, and, what served him better, a mug of spring water. He slept a little now and again, and sometimes he heard her singing to herself as she moved about the house, and so the night wore away. When the sky began to brighten with the dawn he felt for the bag where his little store of money was, and held it out to her, and she took out a bit of copper and a bit of silver money, but she let it drop again as if it was nothing to her, maybe because it was not money she was used to beg for, but food and rags; or maybe because the rising of the dawn was filling her with pride and a new belief in her own great beauty. She went out and cut a few armfuls of heather, and brought it in and heaped it over Hanrahan, saying something about the cold of the morning, and while she did that he took notice of the wrinkles in her face, and the greyness of her hair, and the broken teeth that were black and full of gaps. And when he was well covered with the heather she went out of the door and away down the side of the mountain, and he could hear her cry, "I am beautiful, I am beautiful," getting less and less as she went, till at last it died away altogether.

Hanrahan lay there through the length of the day, in his pains and his weakness, and when the shadows of the evening were falling he heard her voice again coming up the hillside, and she came in and boiled the potatoes and shared them with him the same way as before. And one day after another passed like that, and the weight of his flesh was heavy about him. But little by little as he grew weaker he knew there were some greater than himself in the room with him, and that the house began to be filled with them; and it seemed to him they had all power in their hands, and that they might with one touch of the hand break down the wall the hardness of pain had built about him, and take him into their own world. And sometimes he could hear voices, very faint and joyful, crying from the rafters or out of the flame on the hearth, and other times the whole house was filled with music that went through it like a wind. And after a while his weakness left no place for pain, and there grew up about him a great silence like the silence in the heart of a lake, and there came through it like the flame of a rushlight the faint joyful voices ever and always.

One morning he heard music somewhere outside the door, and as the day passed it grew louder and louder until it drowned the faint joyful voices, and even Winny's cry upon the hillside at the fall of evening. About midnight and in a moment, the walls seemed to melt away and to leave his bed floating on a pale misty light that shone on every side as far as the eye could see; and after the first blinding of his eyes he saw that it was full of great shadowy figures rushing here and there.

At the same time the music came very clearly to him, and he knew that it was but the continual clashing of swords.

"I am after my death," he said, "and in the very heart of the music of Heaven. O Cherubim and Seraphim, receive my soul!"

At his cry the light where it was nearest to him filled with sparks of yet brighter light, and he saw that these were the points of swords turned towards his heart; and then a sudden flame, bright and burning like God's love or God's hate, swept over the light and went out and he was in darkness. At first he could see nothing, for all was as dark as if there was black bog earth about him, but all of a sudden the fire blazed up as if a wisp of straw had been thrown upon it. And as he looked at it, the light was shining on the big pot that was hanging from a hook, and on the flat stone where Winny used to bake a cake now and again, and on the long rusty knife she used to be cutting the roots of the heather with, and on the long blackthorn stick he had brought into the house himself. And when he saw those four things, some memory came into Hanrahan's mind, and strength came back to him, and he rose sitting up in the bed, and he said very loud and clear: "The Cauldron, the Stone, the Sword, the Spear. What are they? Who do they belong to? And I have asked the question this time," he said.

And then he fell back again, weak, and the breath going from him.

Winny Byrne, that had been tending the fire, came over then, having her eyes fixed on the bed; and the faint laughing voices began crying out again, and a pale light, grey like a wave, came creeping over the room, and he did not know from what secret world it came. He saw Winny's withered face and her withered arms that were grey like crumbled earth, and weak as he was he shrank back farther towards the wall. And then there came out of the mud-stiffened rags arms as white and as shadowy as the foam on a river, and they were put about his body, and a voice that he could hear well but that seemed to come from a long way off said to him in a whisper: "You will go looking for me no more upon the breasts of women."

"Who are you?" he said then.

"I am one of the lasting people, of the lasting unwearied Voices, that make my dwelling in the broken and the dying, and those that have lost their wits; and I came looking for you, and you are mine until the whole world is burned out like a candle that is spent. And look up now," she said, "for the wisps that are for our wedding are lighted."

He saw then that the house was crowded with pale shadowy hands, and that every hand was holding what was sometimes like a wisp lighted for a marriage, and sometimes like a tall white candle for the dead.

When the sun rose on the morning of the morrow Winny of the Cross Roads rose up from where she was sitting beside the body, and began her begging from townland to townland, singing the same song as she walked, "I am beautiful, I am beautiful. The birds in the air, the moths under the leaves, the flies over the water look at me. Look at me, perishing woods, for my body will be shining like the lake water after you have been hurried away. You and the old race of men, and the race of the beasts, and the race of the fish, and the winged race, are wearing away like a candle that has been burned out. But I laugh out loud, because I am in my youth."

She did not come back that night or any night to the cabin, and it was not till the end of two days that the turf cutters going to the bog found the body of Red Owen Hanrahan, and gathered men to wake him and women to keen him, and gave him a burying worthy of so great a poet.

My dear A. E.*—I dedicate this book to you because, whether you think it well or ill written, you will sympathize with the sorrows and the ecstasies of its personages, perhaps even more than I do myself. Although I wrote these stories at different times and in different manners, and without any definite plan, they have but one subject, the war of spiritual with natural order; and how can I dedicate such a book to anyone but to you, the one poet of modern Ireland who has moulded a spiritual ecstasy into verse? My friends in Ireland sometimes ask me when I am going to write a really national poem or romance, and by a national poem or romance I understand them to mean a poem or romance founded upon some famous moment of Irish history, and built up out of the thoughts and feelings which move the greater number of patriotic Irishmen. I on the other hand believe that poetry and romance cannot be made by the most conscientious study of famous moments and of the thoughts and feelings of others, but only by looking into that little, infinite, faltering, eternal flame that we call ourselves. If a writer wishes to interest a certain people among whom he has grown up, or fancies he has a duty towards them, he may choose for the symbols of his art their legends, their history, their beliefs, their opinions, because he has a right to choose among things less than himself, but he cannot choose among the substances of art. So far, however, as this book is visionary it is Irish, for Ireland which is still predominantly Celtic has preserved with some less excellent things a gift of vision, which has died out among more hurried and more successful nations: no shining candelabra have prevented us from looking into the darkness, and when one looks into the darkness there is always something there.

W. B. Yeats
London, 1896

---

*A.E. is the pseudonym for George William Russell (1867–1935), Irish poet and mystic. [Ed.]

THE SECRET ROSE

As for living, our servants will do that for us.
—*Villiers de L'Isle Adam.*

Helen, when she looked in her mirror, seeing the withered wrinkles made in her face by old age, wept, and wondered why she had twice been carried away.—*From Leonardo da Vinci's note books.*

TO THE SECRET ROSE

Far off, most secret, and inviolate Rose,
Enfold me in my hour of hours; where those
Who sought thee at the Holy Sepulchre,
Or in the wine-vat, dwell beyond the stir
And tumult of defeated dreams; and deep
Among pale eyelids heavy with the sleep
Men have named beauty. Your great leaves enfold
The ancient beards, the helms of ruby and gold
Of the crowned Magi; and the king whose eyes
Saw the Pierced Hands and Rood of Elder rise
In druid vapour and make the torches dim;
Till vain frenzy awoke and he died; and him
Who met Fand walking among flaming dew,
By a grey shore where the wind never blew,
And lost the world and Emir for a kiss;
And him who drove the gods out of their liss
And till a hundred morns had flowered red
Feasted, and wept the barrows of his dead;
And the proud dreaming king who flung the crown
And sorrow away, and calling bard and clown
Dwelt among wine-stained wanderers in deep woods;
And him who sold tillage and house and goods,
And sought through lands and islands numberless years
Until he found with laughter and with tears
A woman of so shining loveliness
That men threshed corn at midnight by a tress,
A little stolen tress. I too await

The hour of thy great wind of love and hate.
When shall the stars be blown about the sky,
Like the sparks blown out of a smithy, and die?
Surely thine hour has come, thy great wind blows,
Far off, most secret, and inviolate Rose?

THE CRUCIFIXION OF THE OUTCAST

A MAN, WITH thin brown hair and a pale face, half ran, half walked, along the road that wound from the south to the town of Sligo. Many called him Cumhal, the son of Cormac, and many called him the Swift, Wild Horse; and he was a gleeman, and he wore a short parti-coloured doublet, and had pointed shoes, and a bulging wallet. Also he was of the blood of the Ernaans, and his birth-place was the Field of Gold; but his eating and sleeping places were the four provinces of Eri, and his abiding place was not upon the ridge of the earth. His eyes strayed from the Abbey tower of the White Friars and the town battlements to a row of crosses which stood out against the sky upon a hill a little to the eastward of the town, and he clenched his fist, and shook it at the crosses. He knew they were not empty, for the birds were fluttering about them; and he thought how, as like as not, just such another vagabond as himself was hanged on one of them; and he muttered: "If it were hanging or bowstringing, or stoning or beheading, it would be bad enough. But to have the birds pecking your eyes and the wolves eating your feet! I would that the red wind of the Druids had withered in his cradle the soldier of Dathi, who brought the tree of death out of barbarous lands, or that the lightning, when it smote Dathi at the foot of the mountain, had smitten him also, or that his grave had been dug by the green-haired and green-toothed merrows deep at the roots of the deep sea."

While he spoke, he shivered from head to foot, and the sweat came out upon his face, and he knew not why, for he had looked upon many crosses. He passed over two hills and under the battlemented gate, and then round by a left-hand way to the door of the Abbey. It was studded with great nails, and when he knocked at it, he roused the lay brother who was the porter, and of him he asked a place in the guest-house. Then the lay brother took a glowing turf on a shovel, and led the way to a big and naked outhouse strewn with very dirty rushes; and lighted a rush-candle fixed between two of the stones of the wall, and set the glowing turf upon the hearth and gave him two unlighted sods and a wisp of straw, and showed him a blanket hanging from a nail, and a shelf with a loaf of bread and a jug of water, and a tub in a far corner. Then the lay brother left him and went back to his place by the door. And Cumhal the son of Cormac began to blow upon the glowing turf that he might light the two sods and the wisp of straw; but the sods and the straw would not light, for they were damp. So he took off his pointed shoes, and drew the tub out of the corner with the thought of washing the dust of the highway from his feet; but the water was so dirty that he could not see the bottom. He was very hungry, for he had not eaten all that day; so he did not waste much anger upon the tub, but took up the black loaf, and bit into it, and then spat out the bite, for the bread was hard and mouldy. Still he did not give way to his anger, for he had not drunken these many hours; having a hope of heath beer or wine at his day's end, he had left the brooks untasted, to make his supper the more delightful. Now he put the jug to his lips, but he flung it from him straight-way, for the water was bitter and ill-smelling. Then he gave the jug a kick, so that it broke against the opposite wall, and he took down the blanket to wrap it about him for the night. But no sooner did he touch it than it was alive with skipping fleas. At this, beside himself with anger, he rushed to the door of the guest-house, but the lay brother, being well accustomed to such outcries, had locked it on the outside; so he emptied the tub and began to beat the door with it, till the lay brother came to the door and asked what ailed him, and why he woke him out of sleep. "What ails me!" shouted Cumhal, "are not the sods as wet as the sand of the Three Rosses? and are not the fleas in the blanket as many as the waves of the sea and as lively? and is not the bread as hard as the heart of a lay brother who has forgotten God? and is not the water in the jug as bitter and as ill-smelling as his soul? and is not the foot-water the colour that shall be upon him when he has been charred in the Undying Fires?" The lay brother saw that the lock was fast, and went back to his niche, for he was too sleepy to talk with comfort. And Cumhal went on beating at the door, and presently he heard the lay brother's foot once more, and cried out at him, "O cowardly and tyrannous race of friars, persecutors of the bard and the gleeman, haters of life and joy! O race that does not draw the sword and tell the truth! O race that melts the bones of the people with cowardice and with deceit!"

"Gleeman," said the lay brother, "I also make rhymes; I make many while I sit in my niche by the door, and I sorrow to hear the bards railing upon the friars. Brother, I would sleep, and therefore I make known to you that it is the head of the monastery, our gracious abbot, who orders all things concerning the lodging of travellers."

"You may sleep," said Cumhal, "I will sing a bard's curse on the abbot." And he set the tub upside down under the window, and stood upon it, and began to sing in a very loud voice. The singing awoke the abbot, so that he sat up in bed and blew a silver whistle until the lay brother came to him. "I cannot get a wink of sleep with that noise," said the abbot. "What is happening?"

"It is a gleeman," said the lay brother, "who complains of the sods, of the bread, of the water in the jug, of the foot-water, and of the blanket. And now he is singing a bard's curse upon you, O brother abbot, and upon your father and your mother, and your grandfather and your grandmother, and upon all your relations."

"Is he cursing in rhyme?"

"He is cursing in rhyme, and with two assonances in every line of his curse."

The abbot pulled his night-cap off and crumpled it in his hands, and the circular brown patch of hair in the middle of his bald head looked like an island in the midst of a pond, for in Connaught they had not yet abandoned the ancient tonsure for the style then coming into use. "Unless we do not somewhat," he said, "he will teach his curses to the children in the street, and the girls spinning at the doors, and to the robbers upon Ben Bulben."

"Shall I go, then," said the other, "and give him dry sods, a fresh loaf, clean water in a jug, clean foot-water, and a new blanket, and make him swear by the blessed Saint Benignus, and by the sun and moon, that no bond be lacking, not to tell his rhymes to the children in the street, and the girls spinning at the doors, and the robbers upon Ben Bulben?"

"Neither our Blessed Patron nor the sun and moon would avail at all," said the abbot; "for to-morrow or the next day the mood to curse would come upon him, or a pride in those rhymes would move him, and he would teach his lines to the children, and the girls, and the robbers. Or else he would tell another of his craft how he fared in the guest-house, and he in his turn would begin to curse, and my name would wither. For learn there is no steadfastness of purpose upon the roads, but only under roofs and between four walls. Therefore I bid you go and awaken Brother Kevin, Brother Dove, Brother Little Wolf, Brother Bald Patrick, Brother Bald Brandon, Brother James and Brother Peter. And they shall take the man, and bind him with ropes, and dip him in the river that he shall cease to sing. And in the morning, lest this but make him curse the louder, we will crucify him."

"The crosses are all full," said the lay brother.

"Then we must make another cross. If we do not make an end of him another will, for who can eat and sleep in peace while men like him are going about the world? Ill should we stand before blessed Saint Benignus, and sour would be his face when he comes to judge us at the Last Day, were we to spare an enemy of his when we had him under our thumb! Brother, the bards and the gleemen are an evil race, ever cursing and ever stirring up the people, and immoral and immoderate in all things, and heathen in their hearts, always longing after the Son of Lir, and Aengus, and Bridget, and the Dagda, and Dana the Mother, and all the false gods of the old days; always making poems in praise of those kings and queens of the demons, Finvaragh, whose home is under Cruachmaa, and Red Aodh of Cnocna-Sidhe, and Cleena of the Wave, and Aoibhell of the Grey Rock, and him they call Donn of the

Vats of the Sea; and railing against God and Christ and the blessed Saints." While he was speaking he crossed himself, and when he had finished he drew the night-cap over his ears, to shut out the noise, and closed his eyes, and composed himself to sleep.

The lay brother found Brother Kevin, Brother Dove, Brother Little Wolf, Brother Bald Patrick, Brother Bald Brandon, Brother James and Brother Peter sitting up in bed, and he made them get up. Then they bound Cumhal, and they dragged him to the river, and they dipped him in it at the place which was afterwards called Buckley's Ford.

"Gleeman," said the lay brother, as they led him back to the guest-house, "why do you ever use the wit which God has given you to make blasphemous and immoral tales and verses? For such is the way of your craft. I have, indeed, many such tales and verses well nigh by rote, and so I know that I speak true! And why do you praise with rhyme those demons, Finvaragh, Red Aodh, Cleena, Aoibhell and Donn? I, too, am a man of great wit and learning, but I ever glorify our gracious abbot, and Benignus our Patron, and the princes of the province. My soul is decent and orderly, but yours is like the wind among the salley gardens. I said what I could for you, being also a man of many thoughts, but who could help such a one as you?"

"Friend," answered the gleeman, "my soul is indeed like the wind, and it blows me to and fro, and up and down, and puts many things into my mind and out of my mind, and therefore I am called the Swift, Wild Horse." And he spoke no more that night, for his teeth were chattering with the cold.

The abbot and the friars came to him in the morning, and bade him get ready to be crucified, and led him out of the guest-house. And while he still stood upon the step a flock of great grass-barnacles passed high above him with clanking cries. He lifted his arms to them and said, "O great grass-barnacles, tarry a little, and mayhap my soul will travel with you to the waste places of the shore and to the ungovernable sea!" At the gate a crows of beggars gathered about them, being come there to beg from any traveller or pilgrim who might have spent the night in the guest-house. The abbot and the friars led the gleeman to a place in the woods at some distance, where many straight young trees were growing, and they made him cut one down and fashion it to the right length, while the beggars stood round them in a ring, talking and gesticulating. The abbot then bade him cut off another and shorter piece of wood, and nail it upon the first. So there was his cross for him; and they put it upon his shoulder, for his crucifixion was to be on the top of the hill where the others were. A half-mile on the way he asked them to stop and see him juggle for them; for he knew, he said, all the tricks of Aengus the Subtle-hearted. The old friars were for pressing on, but the young friars would see him: so he did many wonders for them, even to the drawing of live frogs out of his ears. But after a while they turned on him, and said his tricks were dull and a shade unholy, and set the cross on his shoulders again. Another half-mile on the way, and he asked them to stop and hear him jest for them, for he knew, he said, all the jests of Conan the Bald, upon whose back a sheep's wool grew. And the young friars, when they had heard his merry tales, again bade him take up his cross, for it ill became them to listen to such follies. Another half-mile on the way, he asked them to stop and hear him sing the story of the White-breasted Deirdre, and how she endured many sorrows, and how the sons of Usna died to serve her. And the young friars were mad to hear him, but when he had ended they grew angry, and beat him for waking forgotten longings in their hearts. So they set the cross upon his back and hurried him to the hill.

When he was come to the top, they took the cross from him, and began to dig a hole to stand it in, while the beggars gathered round, and talked among themselves. "I ask a favour before I die," says Cumhal.

"We will grant you no more delays," says the abbot.

"I ask no more delays, for I have drawn the sword, and told the truth, and lived my vision, and am content."

"Would you, then, confess?"

"By sun and moon, not I; I ask but to be let eat the food I carry in my wallet. I carry food in my wallet whenever I go upon a journey, but I do not taste of it unless I am well-nigh starved. I have not eaten now these two days."

"You may eat, then," says the abbot, and he turned to help the friars dig the hole.

The gleeman took a loaf and some strips of cold fried bacon out of his wallet and laid them upon the ground. "I will give a tithe to the poor," says he, and he cut a tenth part from the loaf and the bacon. "Who among you is the poorest?" And thereupon was a great clamour, for the beggars began the history of their sorrows and their poverty, and their yellow faces swayed like Gara Lough when the floods have filled it with water from the bogs.

He listened for a little, and, says he, "I am myself the poorest, for I have travelled the bare road, and by the edges of the sea; and the tattered doublet of parti-coloured cloth upon my back and the torn pointed shoes upon my feet have ever irked me, because of the towered city full of noble raiment which was in my heart. And I have been the more alone upon the roads and by the sea because I heard in my heart the rustling of the rose-bordered dress of her who is more subtle than Aengus, the Subtle-hearted, and more full of the beauty of laughter than Conan the Bald, and more full of the wisdom of tears than White-breasted Deirdre, and more lovely than a bursting dawn to them that are lost in the darkness. Therefore, I award the tithe to myself; but yet, because I am done with all things, I give it unto you."

So he flung the bread and the strips of bacon among the beggars, and they fought with many cries until the last scrap was eaten. But meanwhile the friars nailed the gleeman to his cross, and set it upright in the hole, and shovelled the earth in at the foot, and trampled it level and hard. So then they went away, but the beggars stayed on, sitting round the cross. But when the sun was sinking they also got up to go, for the air was getting chilly. And as soon as they had gone a little way, the wolves, who had been showing themselves on the edge of a neighbouring coppice, came nearer, and the birds wheeled closer and closer. "Stay, outcasts, yet a little while," the crucified one called in a weak voice to the beggars, "and keep the beasts and the birds from me." But the beggars were angry because he had called them outcasts, so they threw stones and mud at him, and went their way. Then the wolves gathered at the foot of the cross, and the birds flew lower and lower. And presently the birds lighted all at once upon his head and arms and shoulders, and began to peck at him, and the wolves began to eat his feet. "Outcasts," he moaned, "have you also turned against the outcast?"

OUT OF THE ROSE

ONE WINTER EVENING an old knight in rusted chain-armour rode slowly along the woody southern slope of Ben Bulben, watching the sun go down in crimson clouds over the sea. His horse was tired, as after a long journey, and he had upon his helmet the crest of no neighbouring lord or king, but a small rose made of rubies that glimmered every moment to a deeper crimson. His white hair fell in thin curls upon his shoulders, and its disorder added to the melancholy of his face, which was the face of one of those who have come but seldom into the world, and always for its trouble, the dreamers who must do what they dream, the doers who must dream what they do.

After gazing a while towards the sun, he let the reins fall upon the neck of his horse, and, stretching out both arms towards the west, he said, "O Divine Rose of Intellectual Flame, let the gates of thy peace be opened to me at last!" And suddenly a loud squealing began in the woods some hundreds of yards further up the mountain side. He stopped his horse to listen, and heard behind him a sound of feet and of voices. "They are beating them to make them go into the narrow path by the gorge," said someone, and in another moment a dozen peasants armed with short spears had come up with the knight, and stood a little apart from him, their blue caps in their hands.

"Where do you go with the spears?" he asked; and one who seemed the leader answered: "A troop of wood-thieves came down from the hills a while ago and carried off the pigs belonging to an old man who lives by Glen Car Lough, and we turned out to go after them. Now that we know they are four times more than we are, we follow to find the way they have taken;

and will presently tell our story to De Courcey, and if he will not help us, to Fitzgerald; for De Courcey and Fitzgerald have lately made a peace, and we do not know to whom we belong."

"But by that time," said the knight, "the pigs will have been eaten."

"A dozen men cannot do more, and it was not reasonable that the whole valley should turn out and risk their lives for two, or for two dozen pigs."

"Can you tell me," said the knight, "if the old man to whom the pigs belong is pious and true of heart?"

"He is as true as another and more pious than any, for he says a prayer to a saint every morning before his breakfast."

"Then it were well to fight in his cause," said the knight, "and if you will fight against the wood-thieves I will take the main brunt of the battle, and you know well that a man in armour is worth many like these wood-thieves, clad in wool and leather."

And the leader turned to his fellows and asked if they would take the chance; but they seemed anxious to get back to their cabins.

"Are the wood-thieves treacherous and impious?"

"They are treacherous in all their dealings," said a peasant, "and no man has known them to pray."

"Then," said the knight, "I will give five crowns for the head of every wood-thief killed by us in the fighting"; and he bid the leader show the way, and they all went on together. After a time they came to where a beaten track wound into the woods, and, taking this, they doubled back upon their previous course, and began to ascend the wooded slope of the mountains. In a little while the path grew very straight and steep, and the knight was forced to dismount and leave his horse tied to a tree-stem. They knew they were on the right track: for they could see the marks of pointed shoes in the soft clay and mingled with them the cloven footprints of the pigs. Presently the path became still more abrupt, and they knew by the ending of the cloven foot-prints that the thieves were carrying the pigs. Now and then a long mark in the clay showed that a pig had slipped down, and been dragged along for a little way. They had journeyed thus for about twenty minutes, when a confused sound of voices told them that they were coming up with the thieves. And then the voices ceased, and they understood that they had been overheard in their turn. They pressed on rapidly and cautiously, and in about five minutes one of them caught sight of a leather jerkin half hidden by a hazel-bush. An arrow struck the knight's chain-armour, but glanced off harmlessly, and then a flight of arrows swept by them with the buzzing sound of great bees. They ran and climbed, and climbed and ran towards the thieves, who were now all visible standing up among the bushes with their still quivering bows in their hands: for they had only their spears and they must at once come hand to hand. The knight was in the front and struck down first one and then another of the wood-thieves. The peasants shouted, and, pressing on, drove the wood-thieves before them until they came out on the flat top of the mountain, and there they saw the two pigs quietly grubbing in the short grass, so they ran about them in a circle, and began to move back again towards the narrow path: the old knight coming now the last of all, and striking down thief after thief. The peasants had got no very serious hurts among them, for he had drawn the brunt of the battle upon himself, as could well be seen from the bloody rents in his armour; and when they came to the entrance of the narrow path he told them to drive the pigs down into the valley, while he stood there to guard the way behind them. So in a moment he was alone, and, being weak with loss of blood, might have been ended there and then by the wood-thieves had fear not made them begone out of sight in a great hurry.

An hour passed, and they did not return; and now the knight could stand on guard no longer, but had to lie down upon the grass. A half-hour more went by, and then a young lad with what appeared to be a number of cock's feathers stuck round his hat, came out of the path behind him, and began to move about among the dead thieves, cutting their heads off. Then he laid the heads in a heap before the knight, and said: "O great knight, I have been bid come and ask you for the crowns you promised for the heads: five crowns a head. They told me to tell you that they have prayed to God and His Mother to give you a long life, but that they are poor peasants, and that they would have the money before you die. They told me this over and over for fear I might forget it, and promised to beat me if I did."

The knight raised himself upon his elbow, and opening a bag that hung to his belt, counted out the five crowns for each head. There were thirty heads in all.

"O great knight," said the lad, "they have also bid me take all care of you, and light a fire, and put this ointment upon your wounds." And he gathered sticks and leaves together, and, flashing his flint and steel under a mass of dry leaves, had made a very good blaze. Then, drawing off the coat of mail, he began to anoint the wounds: but he did it clumsily, like one who does by rote what he had been told. The knight motioned him to stop, and said: "You seem a good lad."

"I would ask something of you for myself."

"There are still a few crowns," said the knight; "shall I give them to you?"

"O no," said the lad. "They would be no good to me. There is only one thing that I care about doing, and I have no need of money to do it. I go from village to village and from hill to hill, and whenever I come across a good cock I steal him and take him into the woods, and I keep him there under a basket until I get another good cock, and then I set them to fight. The people say I am an innocent, and do not do me any harm, and never ask me to do any work but go a message now and then. It is because I am an innocent that they send me to get the crowns: anyone else would steal them; and they dare not come back themselves, for now that you are not with them they are afraid of the wood-thieves. Did you ever hear how, when the wood-thieves are christened, the wolves are made their godfathers, and their right arms are not christened at all?"

"If you will not take these crowns, my good lad, I have nothing for you, I fear, unless you would have that old coat of mail which I shall soon need no more."

"There was something I wanted: yes, I remember now," said the lad. "I want you to tell me why you fought like the champions and giants in the stories and for so little a thing. Are you indeed a man like us? Are you not rather an old wizard who lives among these hills, and will not a wind arise presently and crumble you into dust?"

"I will tell you of myself," replied the knight, "for now that I am the last of the fellowship, I may tell all and witness for God. Look at the Rose of Rubies on my helmet, and see the symbol of my life and of my hope." And then he told the lad this story, but with always more frequent pauses; and, while he told it, the Rose shone a deep blood-colour in the firelight, and the lad stuck the cock's feathers in the earth in front of him, and moved them about as though he made them actors in the play.

"I live in a land far from this, and was one of the Knights of St. John," said the old man; "but I was one of those in the Order who always longed for more arduous labours in the service of the truth that can only be understood within the heart. At last there came to us a knight of Palestine, to whom the truth of truths had been revealed by God Himself. He had seen a great Rose of Fire, and a Voice out of the Rose had told him how men would turn from the light of their own hearts, and bow down before outer order and outer fixity, and that then the light would cease, and none escape the curse except the foolish good man who could not, and the passionate wicked man who would not, think. Already, the Voice told him, the wayward light of the heart was shining out upon the world to keep the world alive, with a less clear lustre, and that, as it paled, a strange infection was touching the stars and the hills and the grass and the trees with corruption, and that none of those who had seen clearly the truth and the ancient way could enter into the Kingdom of God, which is in the Heart of the Rose, if they stayed on willingly in the corrupted world; and so they must prove their anger against the Powers of Corruption by dying in the service of the Rose of God. While the Knight of Palestine was telling us these things we seemed to see in a vision a crimson Rose spreading itself about him, so that he seemed to speak out of its heart, and the air was filled with fragrance. By this we knew that it was the very Voice of God which spoke to us by the knight, and we told him to direct us in all things, and teach us how to obey the Voice. So he bound us with an oath, and gave us signs and words whereby we might know each other even after many years, and he appointed places of meeting, and he sent us out in troops into the world to seek good causes, and die in doing battle for them. At first we thought to die more readily by fasting to death in honour of some saint; but this he told us was evil, for we did it for the sake of death, and thus took out of the hands of God the choice of the time and manner of our death, and by so doing made His power the less. We must choose our service for its excellence, and for this alone, and leave it to God to reward us at His own time and in His own manner. And after this he compelled us to eat always two at a table to watch each other lest we fasted unduly. And the years passed, and one by one my fellows died in the Holy Land, or in warring upon the evil princes of the earth, or in clearing the roads of robbers; and among them died the knight of Palestine, and at last I was alone. I fought in every cause where the few contended against the many, and my hair grew white, and a terrible fear lest I had fallen under the displeasure of God came upon me. But, hearing at last how this western isle was fuller of wars and rapine than any other land, I came hither, and I have found the thing I sought, and, behold! I am filled with a great joy."

Thereat he began to sing in Latin, and, while he sang, his voice faltered and grew faint. Then his eyes closed, and his lips fell apart, and the lad knew he was dead. "He has told me a good tale," he said, "for there was fighting in it, but I did not understand much of it, and it is hard to remember so long a story."

And, taking the knight's sword, he began to dig a grave in the soft clay. He dug hard, and a faint light of dawn had touched his hair and he had almost done his work when a cock crowed in the valley below. "Ah," he said, "I must have that bird"; and he ran down the narrow path to the valley.

THE WISDOM OF THE KING

THE HIGH-QUEEN OF Ireland had died in childbirth, and her child was put to nurse with a woman who lived in a little house, within the border of the wood. One night the woman sat rocking the cradle, and meditating upon the beauty of the child, and praying that the gods might grant him wisdom equal to his beauty. There came a knock at the door, and she got up, not a little wondering, for the nearest neighbours were in the High-King's house a mile away; and the night was now late. "Who is knocking?" she cried, and a thin voice answered, "Open! for I am a crone of the grey hawk, and I come from the darkness of the great wood." In terror she drew back the bolt, and a grey-clad woman, of a great age, and of a height more than human, came in and stood by the head of the cradle. The nurse shrank back against the wall, unable to take her eyes from the woman, for she saw by the gleaming of the firelight that the feathers of the grey hawk were upon her head instead of hair. But the child slept, and the fire danced, for the one was too ignorant and the other too full of gaiety to know what a dreadful being stood there. "Open!" cried another voice, "for I am a crone of the grey hawk, and I watch over his nest in the darkness of the great wood." The nurse opened the door again, though her fingers could scarce hold the bolts for trembling, and another grey woman, not less old than the other, and with like feathers instead of hair, came in and stood by the first. In a little, came a third grey woman, and after her a fourth, and then another and another and another, until the hut was full of their immense bodies. They stood a long time in perfect silence and stillness, for they were of those whom

61

the dropping of the sand has never troubled, but at last one muttered in a low thin voice: "Sisters, I knew him far away by the redness of his heart under his silver skin"; and then another spoke: "Sisters, I knew him because his heart fluttered like a bird under a net of silver cords"; and then another took up the word: "Sisters, I knew him because his heart sang like a bird that is happy in a silver cage." And after that they sang together, those who were nearest rocking the cradle with long wrinkled fingers; and their voices were now tender and caressing, now like the wind blowing in the great wood, and this was their song:

> Out of sight is out of mind:
> Long have man and woman-kind,
> Heavy of will and light of mood,
> Taken away our wheaten food,
> Taken away our Altar stone;
> Hail and rain and thunder alone,
> And red hearts we turn to grey,
> Are true till Time gutter away.

When the song had died out, the crone who had first spoken, said: "We have nothing more to do but to mix a drop of our blood into his blood." And she scratched her arm with the sharp point of a spindle, which she had made the nurse bring to her, and let a drop of blood, grey as the mist, fall upon the lips of the child; and passed out into the darkness. Then the others passed out in silence one by one; and all the while the child had not opened his pink eyelids or the fire ceased to dance, for the one was too ignorant and the other too full of gaiety to know what great beings had bent over the cradle.

When the crones were gone, the nurse came to her courage again, and hurried to the High-King's house, and cried out in the midst of the assembly hall that the Sidhe, whether for good or evil she knew not, had bent over the child that night; and the king and his poets and men of law, and his huntsmen, and his cooks, and his chief warriors went with her to the hut and gathered about the cradle, and were as noisy as magpies, and the child sat up and looked at them.

Two years passed over, and the king died fighting against the Fer Bolg; and the poets and the men of law ruled in the name of the child, but looked to see him become the master himself before long, for no one had seen so wise a child, and tales of his endless questions about the world and the gods went hither and thither among the houses of the poor. Everything had been well but for a miracle that began to trouble all men; and all women, who, indeed, talked of it without ceasing. The feathers of the grey hawk had begun to grow in the child's hair, and though his nurse cut them continually, in but a little while they would be more numerous than ever. This had not been a matter of great importance, for miracles were a little thing in those days, but for an ancient law of Ireland that none who had any blemish of body could sit upon the throne; and as a grey hawk was a wild thing of the air which had never sat at the board, or listened to the songs of the poets, it was not possible to think of one in whose hair its feathers grew as other than marred and blasted; nor could the people separate from their admiration of the wisdom that grew in him a horror as at one of unhuman blood. Yet all were resolved that he should reign, for they had suffered much from foolish kings and their own disorders, and moreover they desired to watch out the spectacle of his days; and no one had any other fear but that his great wisdom might bid him obey the law, and call some other, who had but a common mind, to reign in his stead.

When the child was seven years old the poets and the men of law were called together by the chief poet, and all these matters weighed and considered. The child had already seen that those about him had hair only, and, though they had told him that they too had had feathers but had lost them because of a sin committed by their forefathers, they knew that he would learn the truth when he began to wander into the country round about. After much consideration they made a new law commanding everyone upon pain of death to mingle artificially the feathers of the grey hawk into his hair; and they sent men with nets and slings and bows into the countries round about to gather a sufficiency of feathers. They decreed also that any who told the truth to the child should be flung from a cliff into the sea.

The years passed, and the child grew from childhood into boyhood and from boyhood into manhood, and from being curious about all things he became busy with strange and subtle thoughts which came to him in dreams, and with distinctions between things long held the same and with the resemblance of things long held different. Multitudes came from other lands to see him and to ask his counsel, but there were guards set at the frontiers, who compelled all that came to wear the feathers of the grey hawk in their hair. While they listened to him his words seemed to make all darkness light and filled their hearts like music; but when they returned to their own lands his words seemed far off, and what they could remember too strange and subtle to help them in their lives. A number indeed did live differently afterwards, but their new life was less excellent than the old: some among them had long served a good cause, but when they heard him praise it, they returned to their own lands to find what they had loved less lovable, for he had taught them how little a hair divides the false and true; others, again, who had served no cause, but built up in peace the welfare of their own households, found their bones softer and their will less ready for toil, for he had shown them greater purposes; and numbers of the young, when they had heard him upon all these things, remembered certain strange words that made all kindly joys and traffic between man and man as nothing, and went different ways, but all into vague regret.

When any asked him about the common things of life; disputes about the meaning of a territory, or about the straying of cattle, or about the penalty of blood; he would turn to those nearest him for advice; but this was held to be from courtesy, for none knew that these matters were hidden from him by thoughts and dreams that filled his mind like the marching and counter-marching of armies. Far less could any know that his heart wandered lost amid throngs of overcoming thoughts and dreams, shuddering at its own solitude.

Among those who came to look at him and to listen to him was the daughter of a little king who lived a great way off; and when he saw her he loved, for she was beautiful, with a beauty unlike the women of his land; but Dana, the great mother, had decreed her a heart that was but as the heart of others, and when she thought of the mystery of the hawk feathers she was afraid. He called her to him when the assembly was over and told her of her beauty, and praised her simply and frankly; and humbly asked her to give him her love, for he was only subtle in his dreams. Overwhelmed with his greatness, she half consented, and yet half refused, for she longed to marry some man who could carry her over a mountain in his arms. Day by day the king gave her gifts; gold enamelled cups and cloths the merchants had carried from India or maybe from China itself; and still she was ever between a smile and a frown; between yielding and withholding. He laid down his wisdom at her feet, and told how the heroes when they die return to the world and begin their labour anew; and a multitude of things that even the Sidhe have forgotten, either because they happened so long ago or because the Sidhe have not time to think of them; and still she half refused, and still he hoped, because he could not believe that a beauty so much like wisdom could hide a common heart.

There was a tall young man in the house who had yellow hair, and was skilled in wrestling; and one day when the king walked in the orchard, which was between the foss and the forest, he heard his voice among the salley bushes which hid the waters of the foss. "My dear," it said, "I hate them for making you weave these dingy feathers into your beautiful hair, and all that the bird of prey upon the throne may sleep easy o' nights"; and then the low, musical voice he loved answered: "My hair is not beautiful like yours; and now that I have plucked the feathers out of your hair I will put my hands through it, thus, and thus, and thus; for it does not make me afraid." Then the king remembered many things that he had forgotten without understanding them, doubtful words of his poets and his men of law, doubts that he had reasoned away; and he called to the lovers in a trembling voice. They came from among the salley bushes and threw themselves at his feet and prayed for pardon, and he stooped down and plucked the feathers out of the hair of the woman and turned away without a word. He went to the hall of assembly, and having gathered his poets and his men of law about him, stood upon the daïs and spoke in a loud, clear voice: "Men of law, why did you make me sin against the laws?

Men of verse, why did you make me sin against the secrecy of wisdom, for law was made by man for the welfare of man, but wisdom the gods have made, and no man shall live by its light, for it and the hail and the rain and the thunder follow a way that is deadly to mortal things? Men of law and men of verse, live according to your kind, and call Eocha of the Hasty Mind to reign over you, for I set out to find my kindred." He then came down among them, and drew out of the hair of first one and then another the feathers of the grey hawk, and, having scattered them over the rushes upon the floor, passed out, and none dared to follow him, for his eyes gleamed like the eyes of the birds of prey; and no man saw him again or heard his voice. Some believed that he found his eternal abode among the demons, and some that he dwelt henceforth with the dark and dreadful goddesses, who sit all night about the pools in the forest watching the constellations rising and setting in those desolate mirrors.

THE HEART OF THE SPRING

A VERY OLD man, whose face was almost as fleshless as the foot of a bird, sat meditating upon the rocky shore of the flat and hazel-covered isle which fills the widest part of Lough Gill. A russet-faced boy of seventeen years sat by his side, watching the swallows dipping for flies in the still water. The old man was dressed in threadbare blue velvet and the boy wore a frieze coat and had a rosary about his neck. Behind the two, and half hidden by trees, was a little monastery. It had been burned down a long while before by sacrilegious men of the Queen's party, but had been roofed anew with rushes by the boy, that the old man might find shelter in his last days. He had not set his spade, however, into the garden about it, and the lilies and the roses of the monks had spread out until their confused luxuriance met and mingled with the narrowing circle of the fern. Beyond the lilies and the roses the ferns were so deep that a child walking among them would be hidden from sight, even though he stood upon his toes; and beyond the fern rose many hazels and small oak trees.

"Master," said the boy, "this long fasting, and the labour of beckoning after nightfall to the beings who dwell in the waters and among the hazels and oak-trees, is too much for your strength. Rest from all this labour for a little to-day for your hand seemed more heavy upon my shoulder and your feet less steady than I have known them. Men say that you are older than the eagles, and yet you will not seek the rest that belongs to age." He spoke eagerly, as though his heart were in the words; and the old man answered slowly and deliberately, as though his heart were in distant days and events.

"I will tell you why I have not been able to rest," he said. "It is right that you should know, for you have served me faithfully these five years, and even with affection, taking away thereby a little of the doom of loneliness which always falls upon the wise. Now, too, that the end of my labour and the triumph of my hopes is at hand, it is the more needful for you to have this knowledge."

"Master, do not think that I would question you. It is for me to keep the fire alight, and the thatch close that the rain may not come in, and strong, that the wind may not blow it among the trees; and to take down the heavy books from the shelves, possessing the while an incurious and reverent heart, for God has made out of His abundance a separate wisdom for everything which lives, and to do these things is my wisdom."

"You are afraid," said the old man, and his eyes shone with a momentary anger.

"Sometimes at night," said the boy, "when you are reading, with the rod of quicken wood in your hand, I look out of the door and see, now a great grey man driving swine among the hazels, and now many little people in red caps who come out of the lake driving little white cows before them. I do not fear these little people so much as the grey man; for, when they come near the house, they milk the cows, and they drink the frothing milk, and begin to dance; and I know there is good in the heart that loves dancing; but I fear them for all that. And I fear the tall white-armed ladies who come out of the air, and move slowly hither and thither, crowning themselves with the roses or with the lilies, and shaking about them their living hair, which moves, for so I have heard them tell each other, with the motion of their thoughts, now spreading out and now gathering close to their heads. They have mild, beautiful faces, Aengus, son of Forbis, but I am afraid of the Sidhe, and afraid of the art which draws them about us."

"Why," said the old man, "do you fear the ancient gods who made the spears of your father's fathers to be stout in battle, and the little people who came at night from the depth of the lakes and sang among the crickets upon their hearths? And in our evil day they still watch over the loveliness of the earth. But I must tell you why I have fasted and laboured when others would sink into the sleep of age, for without your help once more I shall have fasted and laboured to no good end. When you have done for me this last thing, you may go and build your cottage and till your fields, and take some girl to wife, and forget the ancient gods. I have saved all the gold and silver pieces that were given to me by earls and knights and squires for keeping them from the evil eye and from the love-weaving enchantments of witches, and by earls' and knights' and squires' ladies for keeping the people of the Sidhe from making the udders of their cattle fall dry, and taking the butter from their churns. I have saved it all for the day when my work should be at an end, and now that the end is at hand you shall not lack for money to make strong the roof-tree of your cottage and to keep cellar and larder full. I have sought through all my life to find the secret of life. I was not happy in my youth, for I knew that it would pass; and I was not happy in my manhood, for I knew that age was coming; and so I gave myself, in youth and manhood and age, to the search for the Great Secret. I longed for a life whose abundance would fill centuries, I scorned the life of fourscore winters. I would be—no, I *will* be!—like the Ancient Gods of the land. I read in my youth, in a Hebrew manuscript I found in a Spanish monastery, that there is a moment after the Sun has entered the Ram and before he has passed the Lion, which trembles with the Song of the Immortal Powers, and that whosoever finds this moment and listens to the Song shall become like the Immortal Powers themselves; I came back to Ireland and asked the fairy men, and the cow-doctors, if they knew when this moment was; but though all had heard of it, there was none could find the moment upon the hour-glass. So I gave myself to magic, and spent my life in fasting and in labour that I might bring the Gods and the Men of Faery to my side; and now at last one of the Men of Faery has told me that the moment is at hand. One, who wore a red cap and whose lips were white with the froth of the new milk, whispered it into my ear. To-morrow, a little before the close of the first hour after dawn, I shall find the moment, and then I will go away to a southern land and build myself a palace of white marble amid orange trees, and gather the brave and the beautiful about me, and enter into the eternal kingdom of my youth. But, that I may hear the whole Song, I was told by the little fellow with the froth of the new milk on his lips, that you must bring great masses of green boughs and pile them about the door and the window of my room; and you must put fresh green rushes upon the floor, and cover the table and the rushes with the roses and the lilies of the monks. You must do this to-night, and in the morning at the end of the first hour after dawn, you must come and find me."

"Will you be quite young then?" said the boy.

"I will be as young then as you are, but now I am still old and tired, and you must help me to my chair and to my books."

When the boy had left Aengus son of Forbis in his room, and had lighted the lamp which, by some contrivance of the wizard's, gave forth a sweet odour as of strange flowers, he went into the wood and began cutting green boughs from the hazels, and great bundles of rushes from the western border of the isle, where the small rocks gave place to gently sloping sand and clay. It was nightfall before he had cut enough for his purpose, and well-nigh midnight before he had carried the last bundle to its place, and gone back for the roses and the lilies. It was one of those warm, beautiful nights when everything seems carved of precious stones. Sleuth Wood away to the south looked as though cut out of green beryl, and the waters that mirrored it shone like pale opal. The roses he was gathering were like glowing rubies, and the lilies had the dull lustre of pearl. Everything had taken upon itself the look of something imperishable, except a glow-worm, whose faint flame burnt on steadily among the shadows, moving slowly hither and thither, the only thing that seemed alive, the only thing that seemed perishable as mortal hope. The boy gathered a great armful of roses and lilies, and thrusting the glow-worm among their pearl and ruby, carried them into the room, where the old man sat in a half-slumber. He laid armful after armful upon the floor and above the table, and then, gently closing the door, threw himself upon his bed of rushes, to a dream of a peaceful manhood with a desirable wife, and laughing children. At dawn he got up, and went down to the edge of the lake, taking the hour-glass with him. He put some bread and wine into the boat, that his master might not lack food at the outset of his journey, and then sat down to wait until the hour from dawn had gone by. Gradually the birds began to sing, and when the last grains of sand were falling, everything suddenly seemed to overflow with their music. It was the most beautiful and living moment of the year; one could listen to the spring's heart beating in it. He got up and went to find his master. The green boughs filled the door, and he had to make a way through them. When he entered the room the sunlight was falling in flickering circles on the floor and walls and table, and everything was full of soft green shadows. But the old man sat clasping a mass of roses and lilies in his arms, and with his head sunk upon his breast. On the table, at his left hand, was a leather wallet full of gold and silver pieces, as for a journey, and at his right hand was a long staff. The boy touched him and he did not move. He lifted the hands but they were quite cold, and they fell heavily.

"It were better for him," said the lad, "to have said his prayers and kissed his beads!" He looked at the threadbare blue velvet, and he saw it was covered with the pollen of the flowers, and while he was looking at it a thrush, who had alighted among the boughs that were piled against the window, began to sing.

THE CURSE OF THE FIRES
AND OF THE SHADOWS

ONE SUMMER NIGHT, when there was peace, a score of Puritan troopers under the pious Sir Frederick Hamilton, broke through the door of the Abbey of the White Friars at Sligo. As the door fell with a crash they saw a little knot of friars gathered about the altar, their white habits glimmering in the steady light of the holy candles. All the monks were kneeling except the abbot, who stood upon the altar steps with a great brass crucifix in his hand. "Shoot them!" cried Sir Frederick Hamilton, but nobody stirred, for all were new converts, and feared the candles and the crucifix. The white lights from the altar threw the shadows of the troopers up on to roof and wall. As the troopers moved about, the shadows began to dance among the corbels and the memorial tablets. For a little while all was silent, and then five troopers who were the body-guard of Sir Frederick Hamilton lifted their muskets, and shot down five of the friars. The noise and the smoke drove away the mystery of the pale altar lights, and the other troopers took courage and began to strike. In a moment the friars lay about the altar steps, their white habits stained with blood. "Set fire to the house!" cried Sir Frederick Hamilton, and a trooper carried in a heap of dry straw, and piled it against the western wall, but did not light it, because he was still afraid of crucifix and of candles. Seeing this, the five troopers who were Sir Frederick Hamilton's body-guard went up to the altar, and taking each a holy candle set the straw in a blaze. The red tongues of fire rushed up towards the roof, and crept along the floor, setting in a blaze the seats and benches. The dance of the shadows passed away, and the dance of the fires began. The troopers fell back towards the door in the southern wall, and watched those yellow dancers springing hither and thither.

For a time the altar stood safe and apart in the midst of its white light; the eyes of the troopers turned upon it. The abbot whom they had thought dead had risen to his feet and now stood before it with the crucifix lifted in both hands high above his head. Suddenly he cried with a loud voice, "Woe unto all who have struck down those who have lived in the Light of the Lord, for they shall wander among shadows, and among fires!" And having so cried he fell on his face dead, and the brass crucifix rolled down the steps of the altar. The smoke had now grown very thick, so that it drove the troopers out into the open air. Before them were burning houses. Behind them shone the Abbey windows filled with saints and martyrs, awakened, as from a sacred trance, into an angry and animated life. The eyes of the troopers were dazzled, and for a while could see nothing but the flaming faces of saints and martyrs. Presently, however, they saw a man covered with dust who came running towards them. "Two messengers," he cried, "have been sent by the defeated Irish to raise against you the whole country about Manor Hamilton, and if you do not stop them you will be overpowered in the woods before you reach home again! They ride north-east between Ben Bulben and Cashel-na-Gael."

Sir Frederick Hamilton called to him the five troopers who had first fired upon the monks and said, "Mount quickly, and ride through the woods towards the mountain, and get before these men, and kill them."

In a moment the troopers were gone, and before many moments they had splashed across the river at what is now called Buckley's Ford, and plunged into the woods. They followed a beaten track that wound along the northern bank of the river. The boughs of the birch and quicken trees mingled above, and hid the cloudy moonlight, leaving the pathway in almost complete darkness. They rode at a rapid trot, now chatting together, now watching some stray weasel or rabbit scuttling away in the darkness. Gradually, as the gloom and silence of the woods oppressed them, they drew closer together, and began to talk rapidly; they were old comrades and knew each other's lives. One was married, and told how glad his wife would be to see him return safe from this harebrained expedition against the White Friars, and to hear how fortune had made amends for rashness. The oldest of the five, whose wife was dead, spoke of a flagon of wine which awaited him upon an upper shelf; while a third, who was the youngest, had a sweetheart watching for his return, and he rode a little way before the others, not talking at all. Suddenly the young man stopped, and they saw that his horse was trembling. "I saw something," he said, "and yet I do not know but it may have been one of the shadows. It looked like a great worm with a silver crown upon his head." One of the five put his hand up to his forehead as if about to cross himself, but remembering that he had changed his religion he put it down, and said: "I am certain it was but a shadow, for there are a great many about us, and of very strange kinds." Then they rode on in silence. It had been raining in the earlier part of the day, and the drops fell from the branches, wetting their hair and their shoulders. In a little they began to talk again. They had been in many battles against many a rebel together, and now told each other over again the story of their wounds, and so awakened in their hearts the strongest of all fellowships, the fellowship of the sword, and half forgot the terrible solitude of the woods.

Suddenly the first two horses neighed, and then stood still, and would go no further. Before them was a glint of water, and they knew by the rushing sound that it was a river. They dismounted, and after much tugging and coaxing brought the horses to the river-side. In the midst of the water stood a tall old woman with grey hair flowing over a grey dress. She stood up to her knees in the water, and stooped from time to time as though washing. Presently they could see that she was washing something that half floated. The moon cast a flickering light upon it, and they saw that it was the dead body of a man, and, while they were looking at it, an eddy of the river turned the face towards them, and each of the five troopers recognised at the same moment his own face. While they stood dumb and motionless with horror, the woman began to speak, saying slowly and loudly: "Did you see my son? He has upon his head a crown of silver." Then the oldest of the troopers, he who had been most often wounded, drew his sword and said: "I have fought for the truth of my God, and need not fear the shadows of Satan," and with that rushed into the water. In a moment he returned. The woman had vanished, and though he had thrust his sword into air and water he had found nothing.

The five troopers remounted, and set their horses at the ford, but all to no purpose. They tried again and again, and went plunging hither and thither, the horses foaming and rearing. "Let us," said the old trooper, "ride back a little into the wood, and strike the river higher up." They rode in under the boughs, the ground-ivy crackling under the hoofs, and the branches striking against their steel caps. After about twenty minutes' riding they came out again upon the river, and after another ten minutes found a place where it was possible to cross without sinking below the stirrups. The wood upon the other side was very thin, and broke the moon-light into long streams. The wind had arisen, and had begun to drive the clouds rapidly across the face of the moon, so that thin streams of light were dancing among scattered bushes and small fir-trees. The tops of the trees began also to moan, and the sound of it was like the voice of the dead in the wind; and the troopers remembered that the dead in purgatory are said to be spitted upon the points of the trees and upon the points of the rocks. They turned a little to the south, in the hope that they might strike the beaten path again, but they could find no trace of it.

Meanwhile, the moaning grew louder and louder, and the dancing of the moonlight seemed more and more rapid. Gradually they began to be aware of a sound of distant music. It was the sound of a bagpipe, and they rode towards it with great joy. It came from the bottom of a deep, cup-like hollow. In the midst of the hollow was an old man with a red cap and withered face. He sat beside a fire of sticks, and had a burning torch thrust into the earth at his feet, and played an old bagpipe furiously. His red hair dripped over his face like the iron rust upon a rock. "Did you see my wife?" he said, looking up a moment; "she was washing! she was washing!" "I am afraid of him," said the young trooper, "I fear he is not a right man." "No," said the old trooper, "he is a man like ourselves, for I can see the sun-freckles upon his face. We will compel him to be our guide"; and at that he drew his sword, and the others did the same. They stood in a ring round the piper, and pointed their swords at him, and the old trooper then told him that they must kill two rebels, who had taken the road between Ben Bulben and the great mountain spur that is called Cashel-na-Gael, and that he must get up on the horse before one of them and be their guide, for they had lost their way. The piper pointed to a neighbouring tree, and they saw an old white horse ready bitted, bridled, and saddled. He slung the pipe across his back, and, taking the torch in his hand, got upon the horse, and started off before them, as hard as he could go.

The wood grew thinner now, and the ground began to slope up toward the mountain. The moon had already set, but the stars shone brightly between the clouds. The ground sloped more and more until at last they rode far above the woods upon the wide top of the mountain. The woods lay spread out mile after mile below, and away to the south shot up the red glare of the burning town. The guide drew rein suddenly, and pointing upwards with the hand that did not hold the torch, shrieked out, "Look; look at the holy candles!" and then plunged forward at a gallop, waving the torch hither and thither. "Do you hear the hoofs of the messengers?" cried the guide. "Quick, quick! or they will be gone out of your hands!" and he laughed as with delight of the chase. The troopers thought they could hear far off, and as if below them, rattle of hoofs; but now the ground began to slope more and more, and the speed grew more head-long moment by moment. They tried to pull up, but they could not, for the horses seemed to have gone mad. The guide had thrown the reins on to the neck of the old white horse, and was waving his arms and singing in Gaelic. Suddenly they saw the thin gleam of a river, at an immense distance below, and knew that they were upon the brink of the abyss that is now called Lug-na-Gael, or in English the Stranger's Leap. The six horses sprang forward, and five screams went up into the air, a moment later five men and horses fell with a dull crash upon the green slopes at the foot of the rocks.

THE OLD MEN OF THE TWILIGHT

AT THE PLACE, close to the Dead Man's Point, at the Rosses, where the disused pilot-house looks out to sea through two round windows like eyes, a mud cottage stood in the last century. It also was a watchhouse, for a certain old Michael Bruen, who had been a smuggler, and was still the father and grandfather of smugglers, lived there, and when, after nightfall, a tall French schooner crept over the bay from Roughley, it was his business to hang a horn lanthorn in the southern window, that the news might travel to Dorren's Island, and from thence, by another horn lanthorn, to the village of the Rosses. But for this glimmering of messages, he had little business with mankind, for he was very old, and had no thought for anything but for the making of his soul, bent double over his Spanish beads. One night he had watched hour after hour, because a gentle and favourable wind was blowing, and *La Mère de Miséricorde* was much overdue; and he was about to lie down upon his heap of straw, because the dawn was whitening the east, and he knew that she would not dare to round Roughley and come to an anchor after daybreak; when he saw a long line of herons flying slowly from Dorren's Island and towards the pools which lie, half choked with reeds, behind what is called the Second Rosses. He had never before seen herons flying over the sea, for they are shore-keeping birds, and partly because this had startled him out of his drowsiness, and more because the long delay of the schooner had emptied his cupboard, he took down his rusty shot-gun, of which the barrel was tied on with a piece of string, and followed the herons towards the pools.

77

In a little he came upon the herons, of whom there were a great number, standing with lifted legs in the shallow water; and crouching down behind a bank of rushes, looked to the priming of his gun, and bent for a moment over his rosary to murmur: "Patron Patrick, let me shoot a heron; made into a pie it will support me for nearly four days, for I no longer eat as in my youth. If you keep me from missing I will say a rosary to you every night until the pie is eaten." Then he lay down, and, resting his gun upon a large stone, turned towards a heron which stood upon a bank of smooth grass over a little stream that flowed into the pool; for he feared to take the rheumatism by wading, as he would have to do if he shot one of those which stood in the water. But when he looked along the barrel the heron was gone, and, to his wonder and terror, a man of infinitely great age and infirmity stood in its place. He lowered the gun, and the heron stood there with bent head and motionless feathers, as though it had slept from the beginning of the world. He raised the gun, and no sooner did he look along the iron than the old man was again before him, only to vanish when he lowered the gun for the second time. He laid the gun down, and crossed himself three times, and said a *Paternoster* and an *Ave Maria*, and muttered half aloud: "Some enemy of God and of my patron is standing upon the smooth place and fishing in the blessed water," and then aimed very carefully and slowly. He fired, and when the smoke had gone saw an old man, huddled upon the grass, and a long line of herons flying towards the sea. He went round a bend of the pool, and coming to the little stream looked down on a figure wrapped in faded clothes of an ancient pattern and spotted with blood. He shook his head at the sight of so great a wickedness. Suddenly the clothes moved and an arm was stretched upwards towards the rosary which hung about his neck, and long wasted fingers almost touched the cross. He started back, crying: "Wizard, I will let no wicked thing touch my blessed beads"; and the sense of a great danger just escaped made him tremble.

"If you listen to me," replied a voice so faint that it was like a sigh, "you will know that I am not a wizard, and you will let me kiss the cross before I die."

"I will listen to you," he answered, "but I will not let you touch my blessed beads," and sitting on the grass a little way from the dying man, he reloaded his gun and laid it across his knees and composed himself to listen.

"I do not know how many generations ago we, who are now herons, were the men of learning of King Leaghaire; we neither hunted, nor went to battle, nor listened to the Druids preaching, and even love, if it came to us at all, was but a brief trivial thing. The Druids and the poets told us, many a time, of a new Druid Patrick; and most among them were angry with him, while a few thought his doctrine merely the doctrine of the gods set out in new symbols, and were for giving him welcome; but we yawned when they spoke of him. At last they came crying that he was coming to the king's house, and fell to their dispute, but we would listen to neither party, for we were busy with a dispute about the merits of the Great and of the Little Metre; nor were we disturbed when they passed our door with sticks of enchantment under their arms, travelling towards the forest to drive him away, nor when they returned after nightfall with torn coats and despairing cries; for the click of our knives writing our thoughts in Ogham filled us with peace and our dispute filled us with joy; nor even when in the morning crowds passed us to hear the preaching of the new Druid. The crowds passed, and one, who had laid down his knife to yawn and stretch himself, heard a voice speaking far off in the king's house; but our hearts were deaf, and we carved and disputed and read, and laughed together. In a little we heard many feet coming towards the house, and presently two tall figures stood in the door, the one in white, the other in a crimson coat; and we knew the Druid Patrick and our King Leaghaire. We laid down the slender knives and bowed before the king, but it was not the loud rough voice of King Leaghaire that spoke to us, but a voice in which there seemed to be a strange rapture: 'I preached the commandments of God,' it said; 'within the king's house and from the centre of the earth to the windows of Heaven there was a great silence, so that the eagle floated with unmoving wings, and the fish with unmoving fins, while the linnets and the wrens and the sparrows stilled their ever-trembling tongues, and the clouds were like white marble, and the shrimps in the far-off sea-pools became still, enduring eternity in patience, although it was hard.' And as he named these things, it was like a king numbering his people. 'But your slender knives kept up their clicking, and, all else being silent, the sound is not to be endured. Because you have lived where the feet of angels cannot touch you as they pass over your heads, where the hair of demons cannot sweep about you as they pass under your feet, I shall make you an example for ever and ever; you shall become grey herons and stand pondering in grey pools and flit over the world in that hour when it is most full of sighs; and you shall preach to the other herons until they also are like you, and are an example for ever; and your deaths shall come to you by chance and unforeseen, for you shall not be certain about anything for ever and ever.'"

The voice became still, but the voteen bent over his gun with his eyes upon the ground, too stupid to understand what he had heard; and he had remained so, it may be long for a long time, had not a tug at his rosary made him start out of his puzzled dream. The old man of learning had crawled along the grass, and was now trying to draw the cross down low enough for his lips to reach it.

"You must not touch my blessed beads," cried the voteen, and struck the long withered fingers with the barrel of his gun. He need not have trembled, for the old man fell back upon the grass with a sigh and was quiet. He bent down and began to consider the discoloured clothes, for his fear grew less when he understood clearly that he had something the man of learning wanted, and now that the blessed beads were safe, his fear had nearly all gone; and surely, he thought, if that big cloak, and that little tight-fitting shirt under it, were warm and without holes, Saint Patrick would take the enchantment out of them and leave them fit for use. But the old discoloured clothes fell away wherever his fingers touched them, and presently a slight wind blew over the pool and crumbled the old man of learning and all his ancient gear into a little heap of dust, and then made the little heap less and less until there was nothing but the smooth green grass.

WHERE THERE IS NOTHING, THERE IS GOD

ABBOT MALATHGENEUS, BROTHER Dove, Brother Bald Fox, Brother Peter, Brother Patrick, Brother Bittern, Brother Fair-Brows sat about the fire, one mending lines to lay in the river for eels, one fashioning a snare for birds, one mending the broken handle of a spade, one writing in a large book, and one hammering at the corner of a gold box that was to hold the book; and among the rushes at their feet lay the scholars, who would one day be Brothers. One of these, a child of eight or nine years, called Olioll, lay upon his back looking up through the hole in the roof, through which the smoke went, and watching the stars appearing and disappearing in the smoke. He turned presently to the Brother who wrote in the big book, and whose duty was to teach the children, and said, "Brother Dove, to what are the stars fastened?" The Brother, pleased to find so much curiosity in the stupidest of his scholars, laid down the pen and said, "There are nine crystalline spheres, and on the first the Moon is fastened, on the second the planet Mercury, on the third the planet Venus, on the fourth the Sun, on the fifth the planet Mars, on the sixth the planet Jupiter, on the seventh the planet Saturn; these are the wandering stars; and on the eighth are fastened the fixed stars; but the ninth sphere is a sphere made out of the First Substance."

"What is beyond that?" said the child.

"There is nothing beyond that; there is God."

And then the child's eyes strayed to the gold box, and he said, "Why has Brother Peter put a great ruby on the side of his box?"

"The ruby is a symbol of the love of God."

"Why is the ruby a symbol of the love of God?"

"Because it is red, like fire, and fire burns up everything, and where there is nothing, there is God."

The child sank into silence, but presently sat up and said, "There is somebody outside."

"No," replied the Brother. "It is only the wolves; I have heard them moving about in the snow for some time. They are growing very wild, now that the winter drives them from the mountains. They broke into a fold last night and carried off many sheep, and if we are not careful they will devour everything."

"No, it is the footstep of a man, for it is heavy; but I can hear the footsteps of the wolves also."

He had no sooner done speaking than somebody rapped three times.

"I will go and open, for he must be very cold."

"Do not open, for it may be a man-wolf, and he may devour us all."

But the boy had already drawn the bolt, and all the faces, most of them a little pale, turned towards the slowly-opening door.

"He has beads and a cross, he cannot be a man-wolf," said the child, as a man with the snow heavy on his long, ragged beard, and on his matted hair, that fell over his shoulders and nearly to his waist, and upon the tattered cloak that but half-covered his withered brown body, came in and looked slowly from face to face. Standing some way from the fire, and with eyes that had rested at last upon the Abbot Malathgeneus, he said, "O blessed abbot, let me come to the fire and warm myself; that I may not die of the cold and anger the Lord with a wilful martyrdom."

"Come to the fire," said the abbot. "It is a pitiful thing surely that any for whom Christ has died should be as poor as you."

The man sat over the fire, and Olioll took away his now dripping cloak and laid meat and bread and wine before him; but he would eat only of the bread, and he put away the wine, asking for water. When his beard and hair had begun to dry and his limbs had ceased to shiver, he spoke again.

"Set me to some labour, the hardest there is, for I am the poorest of God's poor."

Then the Brothers discussed together what work they could put him to, and at first to little purpose, for there was no labour that had not found its labourer; but at last one remembered that Brother Bald Fox, whose business it was to turn the great quern in the quern-house, for he was too stupid for anything else, was getting old; and so he could go to the quern-house in the morning.

The cold passed away, and the spring grew to summer, and the quern was never idle, nor was it turned with grudging labour, for when any passed the beggar was heard singing as he drove the handle round. The last reason for gloom passed from the brotherhood, for Olioll, who had always been stupid and unteachable, grew clever, and this was the more miraculous because it had come of a sudden. One day he had been even duller than usual, and was beaten and told to know his lesson better in future or be sent into a lower class among little boys who would make a joke of him. He had gone out in tears, and when he came the next day, although his stupidity had so long been the byword of the school, he knew his lesson so well that he passed to the head of the class, and from that day was the best of scholars. At first Brother Dove thought this was an answer to his own prayers and grew proud; but when many far more fervid prayers for more important things had failed, he convinced himself that the child was trafficking with bards, or druids, or witches, and resolved to follow and watch. He had told his thought to the abbot, who told him to come to him the moment he hit the truth; and the next day, which was a Sunday, he stood in the path when the abbot and the Brothers were coming from vespers, and took the abbot by the sleeve and said, "The beggar is of the greatest of saints and of the workers of miracle. I followed Olioll but now, and when he came to the little wood by the quern-house I knew by the path broken in the under-wood and by the foot-marks in the muddy places that he had gone that way many times. I hid behind a bush where the path doubled upon itself at a sloping place, and understood by the tears in his eyes that his stupidity was too old and his wisdom too new to save him from terror of the rod. When he was in the quern-house I went to the window and looked in, and the birds came down and perched upon my head and my shoulders, for they are not timid in that holy place; and a wolf passed by, his right side shaking my habit, his left the leaves of a bush. Olioll opened his book and turned to the page I had told him to learn, and began to cry, and the beggar sat beside him and comforted him until he fell asleep. When his sleep was of the deepest the beggar knelt down and prayed aloud, and said, 'O Thou Who dwellest beyond the stars, show forth Thy power as at the beginning, and let knowledge sent from Thee awaken in his mind, wherein is nothing from the world'; and then a light broke out of the air and I smelt the breath of roses. I stirred a little, and the beggar turned and saw me, and, bending low, said, 'O Brother Dove, if I have done wrong, forgive me, and I will do penance. It was my pity moved me'; but I was afraid and I ran away, and did not stop running until I came here."

Then all the Brothers began talking together, one saying it was such and such a saint, and one that it was not he but another; and one that it was none of these, for they were still in their brotherhoods, but that it was such and such a one; and the talk was near to quarrelling, for each had begun to claim so great a saint for his native province. At last the abbot said, "He is none that you have named, for at Easter I had greeting from all, and each was in his brotherhood; but he is Aengus the Walker to Nowhere. Then years ago he went into the forest that he might labour only with song to the Lord; but the fame of his holiness brought many thousands to his cell, so that a little pride clung to a soul from which all else had been driven. Nine years ago he dressed himself in rags, and from that day nobody has seen him, unless, indeed, it be true that he has been seen living among the wolves on the mountains and eating the grass of the fields. Let us go to him and bow down before him; for at last, after long seeking, he has found the nothing that is God."

PROUD COSTELLO, MACDERMOT'S
DAUGHTER AND THE BITTER TONGUE

COSTELLO HAD COME up from the fields and lay upon the ground before the door of his square tower, resting his head upon his hands and looking at the sunset, and considering the chances of the weather. Though the customs of Elizabeth and James, now going out of fashion in England, had begun to prevail among the gentry, he still wore the great cloak of the native Irish; and the sensitive outlines of his face and his big body had the pride and strength of a simpler age. His eyes wandered from the sunset to where the long white road lost itself over the south-western horizon and to a horseman who toiled slowly up the hill. A few more minutes and the horseman was near enough for his little and shapeless body, his long Irish cloak, and the dilapidated bagpipes hanging from his shoulders, and the rough-haired garron under him, to be seen distinctly in the grey dusk. So soon as he had come within earshot, he began crying: "Is it sleeping you are, Tumaus Costello, when better men break their hearts on the great white roads? Get up out of that, proud Tumaus, for I have news! Get up out of that, you great omadhaun! Shake yourself out of the earth, you great weed of a man!"

Costello had risen to his feet, and as the piper came up to him seized him by the neck of his jacket, and lifting him out of his saddle threw him on to the ground.

"Let me alone, let me alone," said the other, but Costello still shook him.

"I have news from MacDermot's daughter, Una." The great fingers were loosened, and the piper rose gasping.

"Why did you not tell me," said Costello, "that you came from her? You might have railed your fill."

"I have come from her, but I will not speak until I am paid for the shaking."

Costello fumbled at the bag in which he carried his money, and it was some time before it would open, for his hand shook. "Here is all the money in my bag," he said, dropping some French and Spanish money into the hand of the piper, who bit the coins before he would answer.

"That is right, that is a fair price, but I will not speak till I have good protection, for if the MacDermots lay their hands upon me in any boreen after sundown, or in Cool-a-vin by day, I will be left to rot among the nettles of a ditch, or hung where they hung the horse-thieves last Beltaine four years." And while he spoke he tied the reins of his garron to a bar of rusty iron that was mortared into the wall.

"I will make you my piper and my body-servant," said Costello, "and no man dare lay hands upon a man, or upon a dog if he belong to Tumaus Costello."

"And I will only tell my message," said the other, flinging the saddle on the ground, "with a noggin in my hand, and a jug of the Poteen beside me, for though I am ragged and empty, my old fathers were well clothed and full until their house was burnt and their cattle driven away seven centuries ago by the Dillons, whom I shall yet see on the hob of hell, and they screeching."

Costello led him into the rush-strewn hall, where were none of the comforts which had begun to grow common among the gentry, but a mediæval gauntness and bareness, and pointed to the bench in the great chimney; and when the piper had sat down, filled up a horn noggin and set it on the bench beside him, and jug beside that, and lit a torch that slanted out from a ring in the wall; and then turned towards him and said: "Will MacDermot's daughter come to me, Duallach, son of Daly?"

"MacDermot's daughter will not come to you, for her father has set women to watch her, but I am to tell you that this day week will be the eve of St. John and the night of her betrothal to MacNamara of the Lake, and she wants you to be there that, when they tell her to drink to him she loves best, she may drink to you, Tumaus Costello, and let all know where her heart is; and I myself advise you to go with good men about you, for I have seen the horse-thieves with my own eyes." And then he held the now empty noggin towards Costello, and cried: "Fill my noggin again, for I wish the day had come when all the water in the world is to shrink into a periwinkle-shell, that I might drink nothing but Poteen."

Finding that Costello made no reply, but sat in a dream, he burst out: "Fill my noggin, I tell you, for no Costello is so great in the world that he should not wait upon a Daly, even though the Daly travel the road with his pipes and the Costello have a bare hill, an empty house, a horse, and a handful of cows."

"Praise the Dalys if you will," said Costello as he filled the noggin, "for you have brought me a kind word from my love."

For the next few days Duallach went here and there trying to raise a bodyguard, and every man he met had some story of Costello, how he killed the wrestler when but a boy by so straining at the belt that went about them both that he broke the big wrestler's back; how when somewhat older he dragged fierce horses through a ford for a wager; how when he came to manhood he broke the steel horseshoe in Mayo; and of many another deed of his strength and pride; but he could find none who would trust themselves with any so passionate and poor in a quarrel with careful and wealthy persons like MacDermot of the Sheep and MacNamara of the Lake.

Then Costello went out himself, and after listening to many excuses and in many places, brought in a big half-witted fellow, a farm-labourer who worshipped him for his strength, a fat farmer whose forefathers had served his family, and a couple of lads who looked after his goats and cows; and marshalled them before the fire. They had brought with them their heavy sticks, and Costello gave them an old pistol apiece, and kept them all night drinking and shooting at a white turnip which he pinned against the wall with a skewer. Duallach sat on the bench in the chimney playing "The Green Bunch of Rushes," "The Unchion Stream," and "The Princes of Breffeny" on his old pipes, and abusing now the appearance of the shooters, now their clumsy shooting, and now Costello because he had no better servants. The labourer, the half-witted fellow, the farmer and the lads were well accustomed to Duallach's abusiveness, for it was as inseparable from wake or wedding as the squealing of his pipes, but they wondered at the forbearance of Costello, who seldom came either to wake or wedding, and if he had would not have been patient with a scolding piper.

On the next evening they set out for Cool-a-vin, Costello riding a tolerable horse and carrying a sword, the others upon rough-haired ponies, and with their cudgels under their arms. As they rode over the bogs and in the boreens among the hills they could see fire answering fire from hill to hill, from horizon to horizon, and everywhere groups who danced in the red light of the turf. When they came to MacDermot's house they saw before the door an unusually large group of the very poor, dancing about a fire, in the midst of which was a blazing cart-wheel, that circular dance which is so ancient that the gods, long dwindled to be but fairies, dance no other. From the door and through the loop-holes on either side came the light of candles and the sound of many feet dancing a dance of Elizabeth and James.

They tied their horses to bushes, for the number so tied already showed that the stables were full, and shoved their way through a crowd of peasants who stood about the door, and went into the big hall where the dance was. The labourer, the half-witted fellow, the farmer and the two lads mixed with a group of servants who were looking on from an alcove, and Duallach sat with the pipers on their bench, but Costello made his way through the dancers to where MacDermot stood with MacNamara pouring Poteen out of a porcelain jug into horn noggins.

"Tumaus Costello," said the old man, "you have done a good deed to forget what has been, and come to the betrothal of my daughter to MacNamara of the Lake."

"I come," answered Costello, "because when in the time of Costello De Angalo my ancestors overcame your ancestors and afterwards made peace, a compact was made that a Costello might go with his body-servants and his piper to every feast given by a MacDermot for ever, and a MacDermot with his body-servants and his piper to every feast given by a Costello for ever."

"If you come with evil thoughts and armed men," said MacDermot flushing, "no matter how good you are with your weapons, it shall go badly with you, for some of my wife's clan have come out of Mayo, and my three brothers and their servants have come down from the Ox Mountains"; and while he spoke he kept his hand inside his coat as though upon the handle of a weapon.

"No," answered Costello, "I but come to dance a farewell dance with your daughter."

MacDermot drew his hand out of his coat and went over to a pale girl who was now standing but a little way off with her mild eyes fixed upon the ground.

"Costello has come to dance a farewell dance, for he knows that you will never see one another again."

The girl lifted her eyes and gazed at Costello, and in her gaze was that trust of the humble in the proud, the gentle in the violent, which has been the tragedy of woman from the beginning. Costello led her among the dancers, and they were soon drawn into the rhythm of the Pavane, that stately dance which, with the Saraband, the Gallead, and the Morrice dances, had driven out, among all but the most Irish of the gentry, the quicker rhythms of the verse-interwoven, pantomimic dances of earlier days; and while they danced there came over them the weariness with the world, the melancholy, the pity one for the other, the vague anger against common hopes and fears, which is the exultation of love. And when a dance ended and the pipers laid down the pipes and lifted the noggins, they stood a little from the others waiting pensively and silently for the dance to begin again and the fire in their hearts to leap up and to wrap them anew; and so they danced Pavane and Saraband and Gallead and Morrice the night long, and many stood still to watch them, and the peasants came about the door and peered in, as though they understood that they would gather their children's children about them long hence, and tell how they had seen Costello dance with MacDermot's daughter Una, and become by the telling themselves a portion of ancient romance; but through all the dancing and piping MacNamara went hither and thither talking loudly and making foolish jokes that all might seem well, and old MacDermot grew redder and redder, and looked oftener and oftener at the doorway to see if the candles there grew yellow in the dawn.

At last he saw that the moment to end had come, and, in a pause after a dance, cried out that his daughter would now drink the cup of betrothal; then Una came over to where he was, and the guests stood round in a half-circle, Costello close to the wall to the right, and the piper, the labourer, the farmer, the half-witted man and the two farm lads close behind him. The old man took out of a niche in the wall the silver cup from which her mother and her mother's mother had drunk the toasts of their betrothals, and poured Poteen out of a porcelain jug and handed the cup to his daughter with the customary words, "Drink to him whom you love the best."

She held the cup to her lips for a moment, and then said in a clear soft voice: "I drink to my true love, Tumaus Costello."

And then the cup rolled over and over on the ground, ringing like a bell, for the old man had struck her in the face and the cup had fallen, and there was a deep silence.

There were many of MacNamara's people among the servants now come out of the alcove, and one of them, a storyteller and poet, who had a plate and chair in MacNamara's kitchen, drew a French knife out of his girdle and seemed as though he would strike at Costello, but in a moment had been hurled to the ground, his shoulder sending the cup rolling and ringing again. The click of steel had followed quickly, had not there come a muttering and shouting from the peasants about the door and from those crowding up behind them; for all knew that these were no children of Queen's Irish, but of the wild Irish about Lough Gara and Lough Cara, Kellys, Dockerys, Drurys, O'Regans, Mahons, and Lavins, who had left the right arms of their children unchristened that they might give the better blows, and were even said to have named the wolves godfathers to their children.

Costello's hand rested upon the handle of his sword, and his knuckles had grown white, but now he drew his hand away, and, followed by those who were with him, went towards the door, the dancers giving way before him, the most angrily and slowly, and with glances at the muttering and shouting peasants, but some gladly and quickly, because the glory of his fame was over him. He passed through the fierce and friendly peasant faces, and came where his horse and the ponies were tied to bushes; and mounted and made his bodyguard mount also and ride into the narrow boreen. When they had gone a little way, Duallach, who rode last, turned towards the house where a little group of MacDermots and MacNamaras stood next to a bigger group of countrymen, and cried: "MacDermot, you deserve to be as you are this hour, for your hand was always niggardly to piper and fiddler and to poor travelling people." He had not done before the three old MacDermots from the Ox Mountains had run towards their horses, and old MacDermot himself had caught the bridle of a pony belonging to the MacNamaras and was calling to the others to follow him; and many blows and many deaths had been had not the countrymen caught up still blazing sticks from the ashes of the fires and thrown them among the horses with loud cries, making all plunge and rear, and some break from those who held them, the whites of their eyes gleaming in the dawn.

For the next few weeks Costello had no lack of news of Una, for now a woman selling eggs, and now a man or a woman going to the Holy Well, would tell him how his love had fallen ill the day after St. John's Eve, and how she was a little better or a little worse; and the country people still remember how when the night had fallen he would bid Duallach of the Pipes tell out, "The Son of Apple," "The Beauty of the World," "The King of Ireland's Son," or some like tale; and while the world of the legends was a-building, would abandon himself to the dreams of his sorrow.

Costello cared only for the love sorrows, and no matter where the stories wandered, Una alone endured their shadowy hardships; for it was she and no king's daughter who was hidden in the steel tower under the water with the folds of the Worm of Nine Eyes round and about her prison; and it was she who won by seven years of service the right to deliver from hell all she could carry, and carried away multitudes clinging with worn fingers to the hem of her dress; and it was she who endured dumbness for a year because of the little thorn of enchantment the fairies had thrust into her tongue; and it was a lock of her hair, coiled in a little carved box, which gave so great a light that men threshed by it from sundown to sunrise, and awoke so great a wonder that kings spent years in wandering or fell before unknown armies in seeking to discover her hiding-place. There was no beauty in the world but hers, no tragedy in the world but hers; for he was of those ascetics of passion who keep their hearts pure for love or for hatred as other men for God, for Mary and for the Saints.

One day a serving-man rode up to Costello, who was helping his two lads to reap a meadow, and gave him a letter, and rode away; and the letter contained these words in English: "Tumaus Costello, my daughter is very ill. She will die unless you come to her. I therefore command you come to her whose peace you stole by treachery."

Costello threw down his scythe, and sent one of the lads for Duallach, who had become woven into his mind with Una, and himself saddled his horse and Duallach's pony.

When they came to MacDermot's house it was late afternoon, and Lough Gara lay down below them, blue, and deserted; and though they had seen, when at a distance, dark figures moving about the door, the house appeared not less deserted than the Lough. The door stood half open, and Costello knocked upon it again and again, but there was no answer.

"There is no one here," said Duallach, "for MacDermot is too proud to welcome Proud Costello," and he threw the door open, and they saw a ragged, dirty, very old woman, who sat upon the floor leaning against the wall. Costello knew that it was Bridget Delaney, a deaf and dumb beggar; and she, when she saw him, stood up and made a sign to him to follow, and led him and his companion up a stair and down a long corridor to a closed door. She pushed the door open and went a little way off and sat down as before; Duallach sat upon the ground also, but close to the door, and Costello went and gazed upon Una sleeping upon a bed. He sat upon a chair beside her and waited, and a long time passed and still she slept, and then Duallach motioned to him through the door to wake her, but he hushed his very breath, that she might sleep on. Presently he turned to Duallach and said: "It is not right that I stay here where there are none of her kindred, for the common people are always ready to blame the beautiful." And then they went down and stood at the door of the house and waited, but the evening wore on and no one came.

"It was a foolish man that called you Proud Costello," Duallach said at last; "had he seen you waiting and waiting where they left none but a beggar to welcome you, it is Humble Costello he would have called you."

Then Costello mounted and Duallach mounted, but when they had ridden a little way Costello tightened the reins and made his horse stand still. Many minutes passed, and then Duallach cried: "It is no wonder that you fear to offend MacDermot of the Sheep, for he has many brothers and friends, and though he is old, he is a strong and stirring man, and he is of the Queen's Irish, and the enemies of the Gael are upon his side."

And Costello answered flushing and looking towards the house: "I swear by the Mother of God that I will never return there again if they do not send after me before I pass the ford in the Brown River," and he rode on, but so very slowly that the sun went down and the bats began to fly over the bogs. When he came to the river he lingered awhile upon the edge, but presently rode out into the middle and stopped his horse in a shallow. Duallach, however, crossed over and waited on a further bank above a deeper place. After a good while Duallach cried out again, and this time very bitterly: "It was a fool who begot you and a fool who bore you, and they are fools who say you come of an old and noble stock, for you come of whey-faced beggars who travelled from door to door, bowing to serving-men."

With bent head, Costello rode through the river and stood beside him, and would have spoken had not hoofs clattered on the further bank and a horseman splashed towards them. It was a serving-man of MacDermot's, and he said, speaking breathlessly like one who had ridden hard: "Tumaus Costello, I come to bring you again to MacDermot's house. When you had gone, his daughter Una awoke and called your name, for you had been in her dreams. Bridget Delaney the Dummy saw her lips move, and came where we were hiding in the wood above the house and took MacDermot by the coat and brought him to his daughter. He saw the trouble upon her, and bid me ride his own horse to bring you the quicker."

Then Costello turned towards the piper Duallach Daly, and taking him about the waist lifted him out of the saddle and threw him against a big stone that was in the river, so that he fell lifeless into a deep place, and the waters swept over the tongue which had been made bitter, it may be, that there might be a story in men's ears in after time. Then plunging his spurs into the horse, he rode away furiously toward the north-west, along the edge of the river, and did not pause until he came to another and smoother ford, and saw the rising moon mirrored in the water. He paused for a moment irresolute, and then rode into the ford and on over the Ox Mountains, and down towards the sea; his eyes almost continually resting upon the moon. But now his horse, long dark with sweat and breathing hard, for he kept spurring it, fell heavily, throwing him on the roadside. He tried to make it stand up, and failing in this, went on alone towards the moonlight; and came to the sea and saw a schooner lying there at anchor. Now that he could go no further because of the sea, he found that he was very tired and the night very cold, and went into a shebeen close to the shore and threw himself down upon a bench. The room was full of Spanish and Irish sailors who had just smuggled a cargo of wine, and were waiting a favourable wind to set out again. A Spaniard offered him a drink in bad Gaelic. He drank it greedily and began talking wildly and rapidly.

For some three weeks the wind blew inshore or with too great violence, and the sailors stayed drinking and talking and playing cards, and Costello stayed with them, sleeping upon a bench in the shebeen, and drinking and talking and playing more than any. He soon lost what little money he had, and then his long cloak and his spurs and even his boots. At last a gentle wind blew towards Spain, and the crew rowed out to their schooner, and in a little while the sails had dropped under the horizon. Then Costello turned homeward, his life gaping before him, and walked all day, coming in the early evening to the road that went from near Lough Gara to the southern edge of Lough Cay. Here he overtook a crowd of peasants and farmers, who were walking very slowly after two priests and a group of well-dressed persons, certain of whom were carrying a coffin. He stopped an old man and asked whose burying it was and whose people they were, and the old man answered: "It is the burying of Una, MacDermot's daughter, and we are the MacNamaras and the MacDermots and their following, and you are Tumaus Costello who murdered her."

Costello went on towards the head of the procession, passing men who looked angrily at him, and only vaguely understood what he had heard, for now that he had lost the understanding that belongs to good health, it seemed impossible that so much gentleness and beauty could pass away. Presently he stopped and asked again whose burying it was, and a man answered: "We are carrying MacDermot's daughter Una, whom you murdered, to be buried in the island of the Holy Trinity," and the man picked up a stone and threw it at Costello, striking him on the cheek and making the blood flow out over his face. Costello went on scarcely feeling the blow, and coming to those about the coffin, shouldered his way into the midst of them, and laying his hand upon the coffin, asked in a loud voice: "Who is in this coffin?"

The Three Old MacDermots from the Ox Mountains caught up stones and told those about them to do the same; and he was driven from the road, covered with wounds, and but for the priests would have been killed.

When the procession had passed on, Costello began to follow again, and saw from a distance the coffin laid upon a large boat, and those about it get into other boats, and the boats move slowly over the water to Insula Trinitatis; and after a time he saw the boats return and their passengers mingle with the crowd upon the bank, and all scatter by many roads and boreens. It seemed to him that Una was somewhere on the island smiling gently, and when all had gone he swam in the way the boats had been rowed and found the new-made grave beside the ruined Abbey, and threw himself upon it, calling to Una to come to him.

He lay there all that night and through the day after, from time to time calling her to come to him, but when the third night came he had forgotten, worn out with hunger and sorrow, that her body lay in the earth beneath; but only knew she was somewhere near and would not come to him.

Just before dawn, the hour when the peasants hear his ghostly voice crying out, he called loudly: "If you do not come to me, Una, I will go and never return to the island of the Holy Trinity," and before his voice had died away a cold and whirling wind had swept over the island and he saw many figures rushing past, women of the Sidhe with crowns of silver and dim floating drapery; and then Una, but no longer smiling, for she passed him swiftly and angrily, and as she passed struck him upon the face crying: "Then go and never return."

He would have followed, and was calling out her name, when the whole company went up in the air, and, rushing together in the shape of a great silvery rose, faded into the ashen dawn.

Costello got up from the grave, understanding nothing but that he had made his sweetheart angry and that she wished him to go, and wading out into the lake, began to swim. He swam on, but his limbs seemed too weary to keep him afloat, and when he had gone a little way he sank without a struggle.

The next day a fisherman found him among the reeds upon the lake shore, lying upon the white lake sand, and carried him to his own house. And the very poor lamented over him and sang the keen, and when the time had come, laid him in the Abbey on Insula Trinitatis with only the ruined altar between him and MacDermot's daughter, and planted above them two ash-trees that in after days wove their branches together and mingled their trembling leaves.

ROSA ALCHEMICA

O blessed and happy he, who knowing the mysteries of the gods, sanctifies his life, and purifies his soul, celebrating orgies in the mountains with holy purifications.—*Euripides*.

ROSA ALCHEMICA

I

IT IS NOW more than ten years since I met, for the last time, Michael Robartes, and for the first time and the last time his friends and fellow students; and witnessed his and their tragic end, and endured those strange experiences, which have changed me so that my writings have grown less popular and less intelligible, and driven me almost to the verge of taking the habit of St. Dominic. I had just published *Rosa Alchemica*, a little work on the Alchemists, somewhat in the manner of Sir Thomas Browne, and had received many letters from believers in the arcane sciences, upbraiding what they called my timidity, for they could not believe so evident sympathy but the sympathy of the artist, which is half pity, for everything which has moved men's hearts in any age. I had discovered, early in my researches, that their doctrine was no merely chemical phantasy, but a philosophy they applied to the world, to the elements and to man himself; and that they sought to fashion gold out of common metals merely as part of an universal transmutation of all things into some divine and imperishable substance; and this enabled me to make my little book a fanciful reverie over the transmutation of life into art, and a cry of measureless desire for a world made wholly of essences.

I was sitting dreaming of what I had written, in my house in one of the old parts of Dublin; a house my ancestors had made almost famous through their part in the politics of the city and their friendships with the famous men of their generations; and was feeling an unwonted happiness at having at last accomplished a long-cherished design, and made my rooms an expression of this favourite doctrine. The portraits, of more historical than artistic interest, had gone; and tapestry, full of the blue and bronze of peacocks, fell over the doors, and shut out all history and activity untouched with beauty and peace; and now when I looked at my Crevelli and pondered on the rose in the hand of the Virgin, wherein the form was so delicate and precise that it seemed more like a thought than a flower, or at the grey dawn and rapturous faces of my Francesca, I knew all a Christian's ecstasy without his slavery to rule and custom; when I pondered over the antique bronze gods and goddesses, which I had mortgaged my house to buy, I had all a pagan's delight in various beauty and without his terror at sleepless destiny and his labour with many sacrifices; and I had only to go to my bookshelf, where every book was bound in leather, stamped with intricate ornament, and of a carefully chosen colour: Shakespeare in the orange of the glory of the world, Dante in the dull red of his anger, Milton in the blue grey of his formal calm; and I could experience what I would of human passions without their bitterness and without satiety. I had gathered about me all gods because I believed in none, and experienced every pleasure because I gave myself to none, but held myself apart, individual, indissoluble, a mirror of polished steel: I looked in the triumph of this imagination at the birds of Hera, glowing in the firelight as though they were wrought of jewels; and to my mind, for which symbolism was a necessity, they seemed the doorkeepers of my world, shutting out all that was not of as affluent a beauty as their own; and for a moment I thought as I had thought in so many other moments, that it was possible to rob life of every bitterness except the bitterness of death; and then a thought which had followed this thought, time after time, filled me with a passionate sorrow. All those forms: that Madonna with her brooding purity, those rapturous faces singing in the morning light, those bronze divinities with their passionless dignity, those wild shapes rushing from despair to despair, belonged to a divine world wherein I had no part; and every experience, however profound, every perception, however exquisite, would bring me the bitter dream of a limitless energy I could never know, and even in my most perfect moment I would be two selves, the one watching with heavy eyes the other's moment of content. I had heaped about me the gold born in the crucibles of others; but the supreme dream of the alchemist, the transmutation of the weary heart into a weariless spirit, was as far from me as, I doubted not, it had been from him also. I turned to my last purchase, a set of alchemical apparatus which, the dealer in the Rue le Peletier had assured me, once belonged to Raymond Lully, and as I joined the *alembic* to the *athanor* and laid the *lavacrum maris* at their side, I understood the alchemical doctrine, that all beings, divided from the great deep where spirits wander, one and yet a multitude, are weary; and sympathized, in the pride of my connoisseurship, with the consuming thirst for destruction which made the alchemist veil under his symbols of lions and dragons, of eagles and ravens, of dew and of nitre, a search for an essence which would dissolve all mortal things. I repeated to myself the ninth key of Basilius Valentinus, in which he compares the fire of the last day to the fire of the alchemist, and the world to the alchemist's furnace, and would have us know that all must be dissolved before the divine substance, material gold or immaterial ecstasy, awake. I had dissolved indeed the mortal world and lived amid immortal essences, but had obtained no miraculous ecstasy. As I thought of these things, I drew aside the curtains and looked out into the darkness, and it seemed to my troubled fancy that all those little points of light filling the sky were the furnaces of innumerable divine alchemists, who labour continually, turning lead into gold, weariness into ecstasy, bodies into souls, the darkness into God; and at their perfect labour my mortality grew heavy, and I cried out, as so many dreamers and men of letters in our age have cried, for the birth of that elaborate spiritual beauty which could alone uplift souls weighted with so many dreams.

II

My reverie was broken by a loud knocking at the door, and I wondered the more at this because I had no visitors, and had bid my servants do all things silently, lest they broke the dream of my inner life. Feeling a little curious, I resolved to go to the door myself, and, taking one of the silver candlesticks from the mantlepiece, began to descend the stairs. The servants appeared to be out, for though the sound poured through every corner and crevice of the house there was no stir in the lower rooms. I remembered that because my needs were so few, my part in life so little, they had begun to come and go as they would, often leaving me alone for hours. The emptiness and silence of a world from which I had driven everything but dreams suddenly overwhelmed me, and I shuddered as I drew the bolt. I found before me Michael Robartes, whom I had not seen for years, and whose wild red hair, fierce eyes, sensitive, tremulous lips and rough clothes, made him look now, just as they used to do fifteen years before, something between a debauchee, a saint, and a peasant. He had recently come to Ireland, he said, and wished to see me on a matter of importance: indeed, the only matter of importance for him and for me. His voice brought up before me our student years in Paris, and remembering the magnetic power he had once possessed over me, a little fear mingled with much annoyance at this irrelevant intrusion, as I led the way up the wide staircase, where Swift had passed joking and railing, and Curran telling stories and quoting Greek, in simpler days, before men's minds, subtilized and complicated by the romantic movement in art and literature, began to tremble on the verge of some unimagined revelation. I felt that my hand shook, and saw that the light of the candle wavered and quivered more than it need have upon the Mænads on the old French panels, making them look like the first beings slowly shaping in the formless and void darkness. When the door had closed, and the peacock curtain, glimmering like many-coloured flame, fell between us and the world, I felt, in a way I could not understand, that some singular and unexpected thing was about to happen. I went over to the mantlepiece, and finding that a little chainless bronze censer, set, upon the outside, with pieces of painted china by Orazio Fontana, which I had filled with antique amulets, had fallen upon its side and poured out its contents, I began to gather the amulets into the bowl, partly to collect my thoughts and partly with that habitual reverence which seemed to me the due of things so long connected with secret hopes and fears. "I see," said Michael Robartes, "that you are still fond of incense, and I can show you an incense more precious than any you have ever seen," and as he spoke he took the censer out of my hand and put the amulets in a little heap between the *athanor* and the *alembic*. I sat down, and he sat down at the side of the fire, and sat there for a while looking into the fire, and holding the censer in his hand. "I have come to ask you something," he said, "and the incense will fill the room, and our thoughts, with its sweet odour while we are talking. I got it from an old man in Syria, who said it was made from flowers, of one kind with the flowers that laid their heavy purple petals upon the hands and upon the hair and upon the feet of Christ in the Garden of Gethsemane, and folded Him in their heavy breath, until he cried against the cross and his destiny." He shook some dust into the censer out of a small silk bag, and set the censer upon the floor and lit the dust which sent up a blue stream of smoke, that spread out over the ceiling, and flowed downwards again until it was like Milton's banyan tree. It filled me, as incense often does, with a faint sleepiness, so that I started when he said, "I have come to ask you that question which I asked you in Paris, and which you left Paris rather than answer."

He had turned his eyes towards me, and I saw them glitter in the firelight, and through the incense, as I replied: "You mean, will I become an initiate of your Order of the Alchemical Rose? I would not consent in Paris, when I was full of unsatisfied desire, and now that I have at last fashioned my life according to my desire, am I likely to consent?"

"You have changed greatly since then," he answered. "I have read your books, and now I see you among all these images, and I understand you better than you do yourself, for I have been with many and many dreamers at the same cross-ways. You have shut away the world and gathered the gods about you, and if you do not throw yourself at their feet, you will be always full of lassitude, and of wavering purpose, for a man must forget he is miserable in the bustle and noise of the multitude in this world and in time; or seek a mystical union with the multitude who govern this world and time." And then he murmured something I could not hear, and as though to some-one I could not see.

For a moment the room appeared to darken, as it used to do when he was about to perform some singular experiment, and in the darkness the peacocks upon the doors seemed to glow with a more intense colour. I cast off the illusion, which was, I believe, merely caused by memory, and by the twilight of incense, for I would not acknowledge that he could overcome my now mature intellect; and I said: "Even if I grant that I need a spiritual belief and some form of worship, why should I go to Eleusis and not to Calvary?" He leaned forward and began speaking with a slightly rhythmical intonation, and as he spoke I had to struggle again with the shadow, as of some older night than the night of the sun, which began to dim the light of the candles and to blot out the little gleams upon the corner of picture-frames and on the bronze divinities, and to turn the blue of the incense to a heavy purple; while it left the peacocks to glimmer and glow as though each separate colour were a living spirit. I had fallen into a profound dream-like reverie in which I heard him speaking as at a distance. "And yet there is no one who communes with only one god," he was saying, "and the more a man lives in imagination and in a refined understanding, the more gods does he meet with and talk with, and the more does he come under the power of Roland, who sounded in the Valley of Roncesvalles the last trumpet of the body's will and pleasure; and of Hamlet, who saw them perishing away, and sighed; and of Faust, who looked for them up and down the world and could not find them; and under the power of all those countless divinities who have taken upon themselves spiritual bodies in the minds of the modern poets and romance writers, and under the power of the old divinities, who since the Renaissance have won everything of their ancient worship except the sacrifice of birds and fishes, the fragrance of garlands and the smoke of incense. The many think humanity made these divinities, and that it can unmake them again; but we who have seen them pass in rattling harness, and in soft robes, and heard them speak with articulate voices while we lay in death-like trance, know that they are always making and unmaking humanity, which is indeed but the trembling of their lips."

He had stood up and begun to walk to and fro, and had become in my waking dream a shuttle weaving an immense purple web whose folds had begun to fill the room. The room seemed to have become inexplicably silent, as though all but the web and the weaving were at an end in the world. "They have come to us; they have come to us," the voice began again; "all that have ever been in your reverie, all that you have met with in books. There is Lear, his head still wet with the thunderstorm, and he laughs because you thought yourself an existence who are but a shadow, and him a shadow who is an eternal god; and there is Beatrice, with her lips half parted in a smile, as though all the stars were about to pass away in a sigh of love; and there is the mother of the God of humility, he who has cast so great a spell over men that they have tried to unpeople their hearts that he might reign alone, but she holds in her hand the rose whose every petal is a god; and there, O swiftly she comes! is Aphrodite under a twilight falling from the wings of numberless sparrows, and about her feet are the grey and white doves." In the midst of my dream I saw him hold out his left arm and pass his right hand over it as though he stroked the wings of doves. I made a violent effort which seemed almost to tear me in two, and said with forced determination: "You would sweep me away into an indefinite world which fills me with terror; and yet a man is a great man just in so far as he can make his mind reflect everything with indifferent precision like a mirror." I seemed to be perfectly master of myself, and went on, but more rapidly: "I command you to leave me at once, for your ideas and phantasies are but the illusions that creep like maggots into civilizations when they begin to decline, and into minds when they begin to decay." I had grown suddenly angry, and seizing the *alembic* from the table, was about to rise and strike him with it, when the peacocks on the door behind him appeared to grow immense; and then the *alembic* fell from my fingers and I was drowned in a tide of green and blue and bronze feathers, and as I struggled hopelessly I heard a distant voice saying: "Our master Avicenna has written that all life proceeds out of corruption." The glittering feathers had now covered me completely, and I knew that I had struggled for hundreds of years, and was conquered at last. I was sinking into the depth when the green and blue and bronze that seemed to fill the world became a sea of flame and swept me away, and as I was swirled along I heard a voice over my head cry, "The mirror is broken in two pieces," and another voice answer, "The mirror is broken in four pieces," and a more distant voice cry with an exultant cry, "The mirror is broken into numberless pieces"; and then a multitude of pale hands were reaching towards me, and strange gentle faces bending above me, and half wailing and half caressing voices uttering words that were forgotten the moment they were spoken. I was being lifted out of the tide of flame, and felt my memories, my hopes, my thoughts, my will, everything I held to be myself, melting away; then I seemed to rise through numberless companies of beings who were, I understood, in some way more certain than thought, each wrapped in his eternal moment, in the perfect lifting of an arm, in a little circlet of rhythmical words, in dreaming with dim eyes and half-closed eyelids. And then I passed beyond these forms, which were so beautiful they had almost ceased to be, and, having endured strange moods, melancholy, as it seemed, with the weight of many worlds, I passed into that Death which is Beauty herself, and into that Loneliness which all the multitudes desire without ceasing. All things that had ever lived seemed to come and dwell in my heart, and I in theirs; and I had never again known mortality or tears, had I not suddenly fallen from the certainty of vision into the uncertainty of dream, and become a drop of molten gold falling with immense rapidity, through a night elaborate with stars, and all about me a melancholy exultant wailing. I fell and fell and fell, and then the wailing was but the wailing of the wind in the chimney, and I awoke to find myself leaning upon the table and supporting my head with my hands. I saw the *alembic* swaying from side to side in the distant corner it had rolled to, and Michael Robartes watching me and waiting. "I will go wherever you will," I said, "and do whatever you bid me, for I have been with eternal things." "I knew," he replied, "you must need answer as you have answered, when I heard the storm begin. You must come to a great distance, for we were commanded to build our temple between the pure multitude by the waves and the impure multitude of men."

III

I did not speak as we drove through the deserted streets, for my mind was curiously empty of familiar thoughts and experiences; it seemed to have been plucked out of the definite world and cast naked upon a shoreless sea. There were moments when the vision appeared on the point of returning, and I would half-remember, with an ecstasy of joy or sorrow, crimes and hero-isms, fortunes and misfortunes; or begin to contemplate, with a sudden leaping of the heart, hopes and terrors, desires and ambitions, alien to my orderly and careful life; and then I would awake shuddering at the thought that some great imponderable being had swept through my mind. It was indeed days before this feeling passed perfectly away, and even now, when I have sought refuge in the only definite faith, I feel a great tolerance for those people with incoherent personalities, who gather in the chapels and meeting-places of certain obscure sects, because I also have felt fixed habits and principles dissolving before a power, which was *hysterica passio* or sheer madness, if you will, but was so powerful in its melancholy exultation that I tremble lest it wake again and drive me from my new-found peace.

When we came in the grey light to the great half-empty ter-minus, it seemed to me I was so changed that I was no more, as man is, a moment shuddering at eternity, but eternity weep-ing and laughing over a moment; and when we had started and Michael Robartes had fallen asleep, as he soon did, his sleeping face, in which there was no sign of all that had so shaken me and that now kept me wakeful, was to my excited mind more like a mask than a face. The fancy possessed me that the man behind it had dissolved away like salt in water, and that it laughed and sighed, appealed and denounced at the bidding of beings greater or less than man. "This is not Michael Robartes at all: Michael Robartes is dead; dead for ten, for twenty years perhaps," I kept repeating to myself. I fell at last into a feverish sleep, waking up from time to time when we rushed past some little town, its slated roofs shining with wet, or still lake gleam-ing in the cold morning light. I had been too preoccupied to ask where we were going, or to notice what tickets Michael Robartes had taken, but I knew now from the direction of the sun that we were going west-ward; and presently I knew also, by the way in which the trees had grown into the semblance of tattered beggars flying with bent heads towards the east, that we were approaching the western coast. Then immediately I saw the sea between the low hills upon the left, its dull grey broken into white patches and lines.

When we left the train we had still, I found, some way to go, and set out, buttoning our coats about us, for the wind was bitter and violent. Michael Robartes was silent, seeming anxious to leave me to my thoughts; and as we walked between the sea and the rocky side of a great promontory, I realized with a new perfection what a shock had been given to all my habits of thought and of feelings, if indeed some mysterious change had not taken place in the substance of my mind, for the grey waves, plumed with scudding foam, had grown part of a teeming, fantastic inner life; and when Michael Robartes pointed to a square ancient-looking house, with a much smaller and newer building under its lee, set out on the very end of a dilapidated and almost deserted pier, and said it was the Temple of the Alchemical Rose, I was possessed with the phantasy that the sea, which kept covering it with showers of white foam, was claiming it as part of some indefinite and passionate life, which had begun to war upon our orderly and careful days, and was about to plunge the world into a night as obscure as that which followed the downfall of the classical world. One part of my mind mocked this phantastic terror, but the other, the part that still lay half plunged in vision, listened to the clash of unknown armies, and shuddered at unimaginable fanaticisms, that hung in those grey leaping waves.

We had gone but a few paces along the pier when we came upon an old man, who was evidently a watchman, for he sat in an overset barrel, close to a place where masons had been lately working upon a break in the pier, and had in front of him a fire such as one sees slung under tinkers' carts. I saw that he was also a voteen, as the peasants say, for there was a rosary hanging from a nail on the rim of the barrel, and as I saw I shuddered, and I did not know why I shuddered. We had passed him a few yards when I heard him cry in Gaelic, "Idolaters, idolaters, go down to Hell with your witches and your devils; go down to

Hell that the herrings may come again into the bay"; and for some moments I could hear him half screaming and half muttering behind us. "Are you not afraid," I said, "that these wild fishing people may do some desperate thing against you?"

"I and mine," he answered, "are long past human hurt or help, being incorporate with immortal spirits, and when we die it shall be the consummation of the supreme work. A time will come for these people also, and they will sacrifice a mullet to Artemis, or some other fish to some new divinity, unless indeed their own divinities set up once more their temples of grey stone. Their reign has never ceased, but only waned in power a little, for the Sidhe still pass in every wind, and dance and play at hurley, but they cannot build their temples again till there have been martyrdoms and victories, and perhaps even that long-foretold battle in the Valley of the Black Pig."

Keeping close to the wall that went about the pier on the seaward side, to escape the driving foam and the wind, which threatened every moment to lift us off our feet, we made our way in silence to the door of the square building. Michael Robartes opened it with a key, on which I saw the rust of many salt winds, and led me along a bare passage and up an uncarpeted stair to a little room surrounded with bookshelves. A meal would be brought, but only of fruit, for I must submit to a tempered fast before the ceremony, he explained, and with it a book on the doctrine and method of the Order, over which I was to spend what remained of the winter daylight. He then left me, promising to return an hour before the ceremony. I began searching among the bookshelves, and found one of the most exhaustive alchemical libraries I have ever seen. There were the works of Morienus, who hid his immortal body under a shirt of hair-cloth; of Avicenna, who was a drunkard and yet controlled numberless legions of spirits; of Alfarabi, who put so many spirits into his lute that he could make men laugh, or weep, or fall in deadly trance as he would; of Lully, who transformed himself into the likeness of a red cock; of Flamel, who with his wife Parnella achieved the elixir many hundreds of years ago, and is fabled to live still in Arabia among the Dervishes; and of many of less fame. There were very few mystics but alchemical mystics, and because, I had little doubt, of the devotion to one god of the greater number and of the limited sense of beauty, which Robartes would hold an inevitable consequence; but I did notice a complete set of facsimiles of the prophetical writings of William Blake, and probably because of the multitudes that thronged his illumination and were "like the gay fishes on the wave when the moon sucks up the dew." I noted also many poets and prose writers of every age, but only those who were a little weary of life, as indeed the greatest have been everywhere, and who cast their imagination to us, as a something they needed no longer now that they were going up in their fiery chariots.

Presently I heard a tap at the door, and a woman came in and laid a little fruit upon the table. I judged that she had once been handsome, but her cheeks were hollowed by what I would have held, had I seen her anywhere else, an excitement of the flesh and a thirst for pleasure, instead of which it doubtless was an excitement of the imagination and a thirst for beauty. I asked her some question concerning the ceremony, but getting no answer except a shake of the head, saw that I must await initiation in silence. When I had eaten, she came again, and having laid a curiously wrought bronze box on the table, lighted the candles, and took away the plates and the remnants. So soon as I was alone, I turned to the box, and found that the peacocks of Hera spread out their tails over the sides and lid, against a background, on which were wrought great stars, as though to affirm that the heavens were a part of their glory. In the box was a book bound in vellum, and having upon the vellum and in very delicate colours, and in gold, the alchemical rose with many spears thrusting against it, but in vain, as was shown by the shattered points of those nearest to the petals. The book was written upon vellum, and in beautiful clear letters, interspersed with symbolical pictures and illuminations, after the manner of the *Splendor Solis*.

The first chapter described how six students, of Celtic descent, gave themselves separately to the study of alchemy, and solved, one the mystery of the Pelican, another the mystery of the green Dragon, another the mystery of the Eagle, another that of Salt and Mercury. What seemed a succession of accidents, but was, the book declared, the contrivance of preternatural powers, brought them together in the garden of an inn in the South of France, and while they talked together the thought came to them that alchemy was the gradual distillation of the contents of the soul, until they were ready to put off the mortal and put on the immortal. An owl passed, rustling among the vine-leaves overhead, and then an old woman came, leaning upon a stick, and, sitting close to them, took up the thought where they had dropped it. Having expounded the whole principle of spiritual alchemy, and bid them found the Order of the Alchemical Rose, she passed from among them, and when they would have followed was nowhere to be seen. They formed themselves into an Order, holding their goods and making their researches in common, and, as they became perfect in the alchemical doctrine, apparitions came and went among them, and taught them more and more marvellous mysteries. The book then went on to expound so much of these as the neophyte was permitted to know, dealing at the outset and at considerable length with the independent reality of our thoughts, which was, it declared, the doctrine from which all true doctrines rose. If you imagine, it said, the semblance of a living being, it is at once possessed by a wandering soul, and goes hither and thither working good or evil, until the moment of its death has come; and gave many examples, received, it said, from many gods. Eros had taught them how to fashion forms in which a divine soul could dwell, and whisper what they would into sleeping minds; and Ate, forms from which demonic beings could pour madness, or unquiet dreams, into sleeping blood; and Hermes, that if you powerfully imagined a hound at your bedside it would keep watch there until you woke, and drive away all but the mightiest demons, but that if your imagination was weakly, the hound would be weakly also, and the demons prevail, and the hound soon die; and Aphrodite, that if you made, by a strong imagining, a dove crowned with silver and bade it flutter over your head, its soft cooing would make sweet dreams of immortal love gather and brood over mortal sleep; and all divinities alike had revealed with many warnings and lamentations that all minds are continually giving birth to such beings, and sending them forth to work health or disease, joy or madness. If you would give forms to the evil powers, it went on, you were to make them ugly, thrusting out a lip, with the thirsts of life, or breaking the proportions of a body with the burdens of life; but the divine powers would only appear in beautiful shapes, which are but, as it were, shapes trembling out of existence, folding up into a timeless ecstasy, drifting with half-shut eyes, into a sleepy stillness. The bodiless souls who descended into these forms were what men called the moods; and worked all great changes in the world; for just as the magician or the artist could call them when he would, so they could call out of the mind of the magician or the artist, or if they were demons, out of the mind of the mad or the ignoble, what shape they would, and through its voice and its gestures pour themselves out upon the world. In this way all great events were accomplished; a mood, a divinity, or a demon, first descending like a faint sigh into men's minds and then changing their thoughts and their actions until hair that was yellow had grown black, or hair that was black had grown yellow, and empires moved their border, as though they were but drifts of leaves. The rest of the book contained symbols of form, and sound, and colour, and their attribution to divinities and demons, so that the initiate might fashion a shape for any divinity or any demon, and be as powerful as Avicenna among those who live under the roots of tears and of laughter.

IV

A couple of hours after sunset Michael Robartes returned and told me that I would have to learn the steps of an exceedingly antique dance, because before my initiation could be perfected I had to join three times in a magical dance, for rhythm was the wheel of Eternity, on which alone the transient and accidental could be broken, and the spirit set free. I found that the steps, which were simple enough, resembled certain antique Greek dances, and having been a good dancer in my youth and the master of many curious Gaelic steps, I soon had them in my memory. He then robed me and himself in a costume which suggested by its shape both Greece and Egypt, but by its crimson colour a more passionate life than theirs; and having put into my hands a little chainless censer of bronze,

wrought into the likeness of a rose, by some modern crafts-
man, he told me to open a small door opposite to the door by
which I had entered. I put my hand to the handle, but the
moment I did so the fumes of the incense, helped perhaps by
his mysterious glamour, made me fall again into a dream, in
which I seemed to be a mask, lying on the counter of a little
Eastern shop. Many persons, with eyes so bright and still that
I knew them for more than human, came in and tried me on
their faces, but at last flung me into a corner with a little laughter; but all this passed in a moment, for when I awoke my hand
was still upon the handle. I opened the door, and found myself
in a marvellous passage, along whose sides were many divinities wrought in a mosaic, not less beautiful than the mosaic in
the Baptistery at Ravenna, but of a less severe beauty; the
predominant colour of each divinity, which was surely a sym-
bolic colour, being repeated in the lamps that hung from the
ceiling, a curiously-scented lamp before every divinity. I
passed on, marvelling exceedingly how these enthusiasts could
have created all this beauty in so remote a place, and half per-
suaded to believe in a material alchemy, by the sight of so
much hidden wealth; the censer filling the air, as I passed, with
smoke of ever-changing colour.

I stopped before a door, on whose bronze panels were
wrought great waves in whose shadow were faint suggestions
of terrible faces. Those beyond it seemed to have heard our
steps, for a voice cried: "Is the work of the Incorruptible Fire
at an end?" and immediately Michael Robartes answered: "The
perfect gold has come from the *athanor.*" The door swung
open, and we were in a great circular room, and among men
and women who were dancing slowly in crimson robes. Upon
the ceiling was an immense rose wrought in mosaic; and about
the walls, also in mosaic, was a battle of gods and angels, the
gods glimmering like rubies and sapphires, and the angels of the
one greyness, because, as Michael Robartes whispered, they
had renounced their divinity, and turned from the unfolding of
their separate hearts, out of love for a God of humility and sorrow. Pillars supported the roof and made a kind of circular
cloister, each pillar being a column of confused shapes, divinities, it seemed, of the wind, who rose as in a whirling dance of

more than human vehemence, and playing upon pipes and cymbals; and from among these shapes were thrust out hands, and in these hands were censers. I was bid place my censer also in a hand and take my place and dance, and as I turned from the pillars towards the dancers, I saw that the floor was of a green stone, and that a pale Christ on a pale cross was wrought in the midst. I asked Robartes the meaning of this, and was told that they desired "To trouble His unity with their multitudinous feet." The dance wound in and out, tracing upon the floor the shapes of petals that copied the petals in the rose overhead, and to the sound of hidden instruments which were perhaps of an antique pattern, for I have never heard the like; and every moment the dance was more passionate, until all the winds of the world seemed to have awakened under our feet. After a little I had grown weary, and stood under a pillar watching the coming and going of those flame-like figures; until gradually I sank into a half-dream, from which I was awakened by seeing the petals of the great rose, which had no longer the look of mosaic, falling slowly through the incense-heavy air, and, as they fell, shaping into the likeness of living beings of an extraordinary beauty. Still faint and cloud-like, they began to dance, and as they danced took a more and more definite shape, so that I was able to distinguish beautiful Grecian faces and august Egyptian faces, and now and again to name a divinity by the staff in his hand or by a bird fluttering over his head; and soon every mortal foot danced by the white foot of an immortal; and in the troubled eyes that looked into untroubled shadowy eyes, I saw the brightness of uttermost desire as though they had found at length, after unreckonable wandering, the lost love of their youth. Sometimes, but only for a moment, I saw a faint solitary figure with a veiled face, and carrying a faint torch, flit among the dancers, but like a dream within a dream, like a shadow of a shadow, and I knew by an understanding born from a deeper fountain than thought, that it was Eros himself, and that his face was veiled because no man or woman from the beginning of the world has ever known what love is, or looked into his eyes, for Eros alone of divinities is altogether a spirit, and hides in passions not of his essence if he would commune with a mortal heart. So that if a man love nobly he knows love through infinite pity, unspeakable trust, unending sympathy; and if ignobly through vehement jealousy, sudden hatred, and unappeasable desire; but unveiled love he never knows. While I thought these things, a voice cried to me from the crimson figures: "Into the dance! there is none that can be spared out of the dance; into the dance! into the dance! that the gods may make them bodies out of the substance of our hearts"; and before I could answer, a mysterious wave of passion, that seemed like the soul of the dance moving within our souls, took hold of me, and I was swept, neither consenting nor refusing, into the midst. I was dancing with an immortal august woman, who had black lilies in her hair, and her dreamy gesture seemed laden with a wisdom more profound than the darkness that is between star and star, and with a love like the love that breathed upon the waters; and as we danced on and on, the incense drifted over us and round us, covering us away as in the heart of the world, and ages seemed to pass, and tempests to awake and perish in the folds of our robes and in her heavy hair.

Suddenly I remembered that her eyelids had never quivered, and that her lilies had not dropped a black petal, or shaken from their places, and understood with a great horror that I danced with one who was more or less than human, and who was drinking up my soul as an ox drinks up a wayside pool; and I fell, and darkness passed over me.

V

I awoke suddenly as though something had awakened me, and saw that I was lying on a roughly painted floor, and that on the ceiling, which was at no great distance, was a roughly painted rose, and about me on the walls half-finished paintings. The pillars and the censers had gone; and near me a score of sleepers lay wrapped in disordered robes, their upturned faces looking to my imagination like hollow masks; and a chill dawn was shining down upon them from a long window I had not noticed before; and outside the sea roared. I saw Michael Robartes lying at a little distance and beside him an overset bowl of wrought bronze which looked as though it had once held incense. As I sat thus, I heard a sudden tumult of angry men and women's voices mix with the roaring of the sea; and leaping to my feet, I went quickly to Michael Robartes, and tried to shake him out of his sleep. I then seized him by the shoulder and tried to lift him, but he fell backwards, and sighed faintly; and the voices became louder and angrier; and there was a sound of heavy blows upon the door, which opened on to the pier. Suddenly I heard a sound of rending wood, and I knew it had begun to give, and I ran to the door of the room. I pushed it open and came out upon a passage whose bare boards clattered under my feet, and found in the passage another door which led into an empty kitchen; and as I passed through the door I heard two crashes in quick succession, and knew by the sudden noise of feet and the shouts that the door which opened on to the pier had fallen inwards. I ran from the kitchen and out into a small yard, and from this down some steps which descended the seaward and sloping side of the pier, and from the steps clambered along the water's edge, with the angry voices ringing in my ears. This part of the pier had been but lately refaced with blocks of granite, so that it was almost clear of seaweed; but when I came to the old part, I found it so slippery with green weed that I had to climb up on to the roadway. I looked towards the Temple of the Alchemical Rose, where the fishermen and the women were still shouting, but somewhat more faintly, and saw that there was no one about the door or upon the pier; but as I looked, a little crowd hurried out of the door and began gathering large stones from where they were heaped up in readiness for the next time a storm shattered the pier, when they would be laid under blocks of granite. While I stood watching the crowd, an old man, who was, I think, the voteen, pointed to me, and screamed out something, and the crowd whitened, for all the faces had turned towards me. I ran, and it was well for me that pullers of the oar are poorer men with their feet than with their arms and their bodies; and yet while I ran I scarcely heard the following feet or the angry voices, for many voices of exultation and lamentation, which were forgotten as a dream is forgotten the moment they were heard, seemed to be ringing in the air over my head.

There are moments even now when I seem to hear those voices of exultation and lamentation, and when the indefinite world, which has but half lost its mastery over my heart and my intellect, seems about to claim a perfect mastery; but I carry the rosary about my neck, and when I hear, or seem to hear them, I press it to my heart and say: "He whose name is Legion is at our doors deceiving our intellects with subtlety and flattering our hearts with beauty, and we have no trust but in Thee"; and then the war that rages within me at other times is still, and I am at peace.